In My Whi
(With Black Curtains Near the Station)

John Arthur Cooper.

It is recommended that the following books published by the author are read prior to this book

(1) Subject To Status. / sequel - Black Nothing.
(2) The Ten Bob Notes. / sequel - When Jonny Comes Marching Home.

Chapter 1.

Calypso Fortnum stood with a gin in her hand in front of the tall elegant window looking at the rain running down the imperfect glass.

Her husband Jolyon gone, disappeared in a jet plane that no one would talk about. Her lover Jonny gone, by his own hand in some seedy little back street house in Walsall for God knows what reason. Even that she'd only found out from Lady Edwina when Salvador was being delivered to Bovington for the summer holidays. Apparently the heartbroken Veronica and the bookish Hetty had turned up at the hall after the payments to Hetty's women's refuge charity had suddenly stopped.

Her son Salvador whisked away by Sir Baltimore, Lady Edwina and their money at the earliest possible moment to be educated and trained to be the best. To replace her husband but not for her. For the bloody estate, an heir to the money.

Mother locked in her room not knowing who anybody was and hiding shitty knickers under her mattress or in the drawers. Calypso had never known mother wash her hair, she insisted it was perfect just the way it was.

Her father? Who knows? Thin and lanky with a big cock and rastafarian dreadlocks lounging in some hovel puffing away at ganja and blurting out 'no worries' to every question on some Carribean island.

Her 'official' father, Captain Benjamin Levington Guinness had recently died of a sudden heart attack. He'd been complaining of pains and palpitations for years so it was no surprise, and if she was honest she didn't miss him. They'd never been close, she was just an accepted liability conceived by a moment of sheer animal passion and lust on a Caribbean island during their strange honeymoon. No, she couldn't remember him ever kissing her.

Everything was perfect, she thought back to the day when she'd watched Jonny's little blue sports car trundle away up the long and winding road til it just disappeared, til he disappeared never to be seen again. Or so real life told her. The gin or whisky definitely helped, sometimes if she drank enough she'd go to a place where she could see Jolyon and Jonny, two chums happy as larry but they just wouldn't talk to her.

There was always a full decanter of decent Irish whisky in her bedroom, it was necessary for sleep. Calypso stood in front of the mirror in her underwear. Her tiny waist had disappeared long ago, replaced by rolls of boredom and feelings of futility. Her arse, which a few years ago could guarantee attention was now wider, bigger, fatter. Her breasts were bigger but then again so was she. Her curly dangling shiny hair still looked OK but required a lot more effort. Calypso emptied the glass and got into bed. Tomorrow she'd stop, she'd get a job, any job, a cleaner, a shop assistant, anything other than nothing.

A maid came into her room to pick up her clothes, take away some and hang up others.

The little green Lotus Elan lingered and hid in the corner of the large garage. The hood was down and everything was covered in dust. It hadn't moved a wheel in fifteen years. The Captain had insisted that if she drove at all she drove the Range Rover, at least it was big if she hit anything. Deep down she knew it wasn't about her, it was about Salvador. He was heir to his fortune as well as the Clay's. There was a driver for the Rover, he had told her his name but she couldn't remember it. He seemed a nice man but there was something 'military' about him. Maybe his name was 'Tommy', yes that was it.

"Tommy."
"Yes Ma'am."
"Tommy, I want you to spruce up my old green sports car, you know, clean it up, get it some new tyres, get it going again so I can use it."
"Is that wise Ma'am? You know the Captain didn't like you driving."
"The Captain's dead Tommy. Sort my car out please. I need to get my life back."
"Yes Ma'am."

Chapter 2.

Slowly the light began to coalesce into shapes of dark and light areas, then there was this frizzy light brown leaning to ginger head of hair with a round pink face under it.

"Am I dead?" It was the first words he'd spoken for nearly a week.

"No, you're bloody well not. You're in the Royal Vic in sunny Newcastle."

"Sandra! Sandra, is it really you? Have you saved my life?" Joel croaked.

"Yes it's me and yes I've saved your life so you owe me one pretty boy."

"How long have I been here?"

"About a week, the doctors have kept you heavily sedated to give your body a chance to wean itself off the gear. How on earth did somebody as smart as you get in such a mess."

"It's a long story, I'll write a book about it one day. Just never trust a woman in a very short skirt and no knickers."

"Well I've got pants not knickers and blue jeans so you can trust me."

Joel turned his head to look directly into her eyes.

"I know that Sandra. Thank you."

He tried to lift his head but couldn't, a week of lying in the hospital bed had dissolved his muscles.

"Help me up Sandra, i want to sit up?"

Sandra put her strong arm around him and built a pillow wall behind him.

"So, what happened?" Joel weakly asked.

"Well I got this strange phone call from this OD'd bloke about eleven one dark cold night, calling out my name before the line went dead, did '147-1' got the number then rang '999' for the police. Told them there was someone probably dying at that number and the rest is history."

"But you live in Essex?"

"Wow you remember something about me then."

"Oh for Gods sake you're always going to be part of my life, we both know that."

"Yeah! Me always hanging around waiting to pick up the pieces. I'm pathetic!"

"No you're not, you're wonderful. The women I fall in love with all seem to die off."

"You're not in love with me then?"

"I love you Sandra, I'm not 'in-love' with you. That's much better, that's for life."

"Yeah well your's wouldn't have been very long if it hadn't been for me. Just you remember that." She leant over and kissed his forehead.

"What you doing these days anyway?" Joel asked.

"A degree at Bristol Uni."

"What in?"

"Mammalogy, want to be a vet."

"Are you happy?"

"Very."

"Anybody special?"

Sandra looked at him.

"Look at me Joel, I'm fat with ginger frizzy hair and a round pink face. What do you think?"

"I'm not special then?"

"You. Leonard Flower Joel, very nearly died, now lie back and rest."

"How do you know my new name?"

"It says so on the end of your bed."

"Oh! What happens now Sandra?"

"Well apparently you're booked in on one the first seats in a spaceship to Mars. How the bloody hell should I know."

A starched nurse bustled into the room except it wasn't quite a room just the corner of a ward that had been partitioned off.

"Well Well Well! Mr. Joel. it's amazing what a pretty girl can do."

Sandra looked at Joel and then the nurse.

"Why, who else has visited him?" Sandra questioned.

The nurse ignored her.

"Speaking of visitors, there's a Mr. Edenson coming to visit you the day after tomorrow so it's a good job you're *Compos Mentis* as it were." After writing on the clipboard she left.

"You've just sunk to a new low. Who's he?" Sandra asked.

"He's a man I know, well I don't actually know him, I've interacted with him on a couple of occasions."

"Interacted? Interacted? What the hell does that mean? Is he your dealer?"

"Well i suppose you could call him that but not for what you think. I do usually end up doing a deal with him, not particularly good or nice ones but a deal nevertheless."

"Just tell him to 'F' off then."

"There's usually some money in it for me Sandra and at the moment I haven't got any. How long you going to stay with me?"

"Got to go back tonight, got some work I've got to submit by the end of the week."

"How will I manage without you?"

"Get one of the nurses to give you a wank, they're prettier than me."

"Can't you do it?"

Sandra looked around then slid her hand under the sheets. She'd never touched him before. Joel sunk back into the pillow his eyes closed as her strong hand closed on him. She seemed to know exactly where to rub, how to make him do anything she wanted. It didn't take long before her hand and the sheet were wet.

"Feel better?" Joel's breathing had increased but was now subsiding.

Sandra took out her hand and wiped it on a tissue.

"Put your hand back will you? Hold me til I'm hard again. I just want to feel you."

She slid her hand under the damp sheet and held him whilst she sat and he lay in silence.

Chapter 3.

The sun was shining which was unusual for this time of the year. Calypso felt like shit She'd seen off at least half a bottle of whisky last night. It was ten years to the day or rather night when Jolyon hadn't come home. The dreadful feeling had never left her, the deep suspicion that it was all that horrible Hetty's fault had never left her, encouraging him to get involved in all that socialist rubbish. The world wasn't a fair or nice place, it never would be, there'd always be rich and poor, smart and stupid, soft and hard, givers and takers. She was convinced Henrietta Betts had taken her husband and maybe even her lover.

She'd felt so lonely, last night she'd made an unscheduled call to Salvador. She usually rang him on Monday and Friday nights but last night was Wednesday, it was a bit hit and miss, she had to ring the phone box in the town, hope somebody answered then get that somebody to go and get him. There were usually boys hanging around the phone box. She just needed to speak to her beautiful boy, hear his voice, tell him she loved him. He wasn't particularly pleased, he could tell she was drunk, he said so. Eton wasn't the best place to have a drunk for a mother, especially one who looked as though she should be cooking 'Jerk' chicken on a tropical island.

A knock came at the door. It was Tommy, she knew his knock. She didn't open it.

"Your car's ready Ma'am. It's around the back."
"Is the hood up or down Tommy?"
"Down Ma'am."
"I'll be down in an hour."
"Yes Ma'am."

Tommy knew she needed time to get herself together, Shower and dress, eat and drink something without alcohol.

Calypso was excited about driving her little Elan again. She remembered the day she'd shoehorned her 'official' father into it before driving off to the little church with a thatched roof to marry Jolyon. Her childhood friend, her love, but not her lover. He was 'Best Man' and always would be. Now all she had left was memories, her little green sports car and her darling son.

Tommy was waiting for her by the car.

"There she is Ma'am, all spick and span and ready to go. Didn't need much, four new tyres, the clutch was seized, and the brakes needed freeing but that was about it. Tank of fresh petrol and a decent battery and she fired up no problem."

Calypso opened the drivers door and got in. As a young girl she just used to effortlessly slip into the driver's seat, her legs unconsciously falling into place on the pedals, now they required some effort to bend and find them. The seat seemed smaller, the thin wooden steering wheel somehow seemed like a toy in her hands.

"Are you OK to drive it Ma'am?"
"Of course Tommy. I'm going to use it all the time from now on, fed up of being chauffeured around in the bloody Range Rover."

She pumped the accelerator twice and turned the key, the engine jumped into raucous eager life, she revved it a couple of times and smiled at Tommy.

"What's the weather forecast Tommy, is it going to rain?"
"Clouding over this afternoon Ma'am but no rain."
"I'm going to drive down to Wicklow and visit the Black Castle."
"It's hardly a castle Ma'am just a few old stones on a rock."
"Nothing in life is ever what you want it to be Tommy."
"What about love?"
"It's never equal is it? One always loves more than the other."

She pressed the clutch and gently pushed the gearstick forward into first gear. The knob was wood with a yellow Lotus badge on the top. The car had only ever done about twenty thousand miles so the synchromesh still worked. She drove carefully out of the back courtyard of Luggala, feeling more comfortable, more confident, with each ascending gear. It felt so good, so free, so joyful.

Within five miles it had all come back, the little car had it's own spirit, the engine pulling like a puppy on a leash, the new tyres and soft suspension soaking up the imperfections of the road, the steering sent it where she wanted to go.

Villages and small towns were simply places to show off, as she complied with speed limits simply so people could look at her. In the Rover she'd just ignore them but this was fun. The sun made her moving hair shine. She'd paid special attention to her make up this morning, more eye makeup than usual. Tommy had noticed but he hadn't said anything.

Then it was there, stretching into forever, the shimmering water of the sea. It always amazed her that once on the water you could go anywhere in the world, there were no borders, no obstacles, no impediments to stop her. If she could sail, she could sail to China, she didn't need a ticket or a passport. When she travelled in the helicopter the sea and the little boats on it always fascinated her.

They'd told her that Jolyon's plane had gone down in the North Sea, perhaps she should just drive off the jetty and join him. Irish Sea, North Sea, Atlantic, Pacific, it was just water, perhaps he was waiting for her.

Calypso pushed those thoughts from her mind, telling herself that Salvador needed her, - but only if she was sober. She added her own caveat.

Ice creams always tasted better when looking out to sea in the sunshine, someone to share it with would have been nice. Tommy was right, it was barely a castle just a few mounds of old stone poking out of the grass on a rocky outcrop. A young couple sat very much together on the rock ten yards to her right. To them Calypso was invisible.

She had no idea if Jonny had been buried or cremated. If he was buried she could at least visit his grave. Veronica would know, it was obvious that she had been head over heels in love with him. Calypso licked up the dribbles on the side of her cornet. Perhaps she should try to lose some weight, start going to a few parties again, look for someone. Then again how could she replace Jolyon? Her childhood playmate, a jet fighter pilot, her husband, men like that only come round once in a lifetime. Then Jonny, a gifted talented man from the wrong side of the tracks who took her to another place, made her float with physical passion, made her abandon every inhibition or convention she knew. It was an irreplaceable combination; no, her life was over, her flower was dying, there were no bees buzzing around it.

Walking back to her car made her smile again. At least he'd sat in it, moaning at her to slow down as she laughed her way around the next bend, confident that the little car would do as she asked.

The road through the Wicklow mountains was just made for the Lotus.

Calypso caressed the car through the shallow bends and directed it through the tight ones. She hadn't had such fun for years. She looked at herself in the small dash mounted rear view mirror. She didn't look too----------.

The tractor and trailer just pulled out without even slowing or looking. There was no time or space to do anything.

"Am I dead?" The weak voiced question was directed to Michael O'Brien who was standing at the foot of her bed in what could be taken for a five star hotel room except that there was medical stuff in it.

"No Not quite."

O'Brien could be mistaken for a congenial, friendly grandfather but it would be a mistake. A staunch and strict Catholic. One time Estate Agent for Luggala, sometimes a solicitor, oft times a drinking partner for the Captain, now co-executor of the estate along with Calypso until Salvador came of age. Full time very dangerous shark with a lot of dodgy contacts.

Michael O'Brien didn't like, or approve of Calypso Fortnum-Guinness but hid it well. He viewed her as a 'bastard' liability he had to manage.

"Where's my car?"
"What on earth do you want to know that for, that's the least of your worries. What's left of it is back in the garage at Luggala, where it should have bloody well stayed. You've been sedated for the last four days, not for medical reasons but to stop the police taking a fucking blood sample from you. We've told them that it's touch and go whether you make it or not so when they get round to interviewing you make sure you stick to that line."
"I hadn't touched a drop that day. I would have been fine."
"Calypso, the staff informed me that you'd drank nearly a whole bottle of BushMills finest the night before. There'd be more alcohol than blood."
"I felt bad, it was ten years to the day Jolyon died."

Michael softened slightly.

"Oh, Sorry to hear that." There was a hesitant pause. "We think you should try and get some professional help, - there's no other way to say it - for your drink problem."
"What problem? And who the bloody hell are we?"
"Me and Delph and there is a problem. We'd like you to go away to a rehab for a few months. A different environment, different people."

Calypso struggled to sit up. She caught sight of herself in the mirror above the wash basin. Her perfect olive skinned face was a bloated and bruised black and blue. She reached up and touched it. It hurt, it was painful.

"What's happened to my face? I had the seat belt on."
"You didn't go through the windscreen Calypso, the screen came at you. It's a bloody plastic car for God's sake. Why did you think the Captain insisted you drove the Rover. The idiot boy driving the tractor and trailer was only fourteen, they haven't got the sense they were born with at that age."

"Tell the police I don't want to make any complaint, pay out for any damage to the tractor and don't bother with any insurance claim for my car. They'd only write it off and I don't want that. Tommy can repair it. It'll give him something to do."

Michael O'Brien looked unbelievably at her.

"What else have I got?" Calypso moaned.
"A broken right ankle, a crushed left ankle and some broken ribs."

Calypso sank back into her pillows.

"I'm not going to any bloody rehab, you can forget that, load of do gooding quacks, talking therapies and fake flower smells. It's just a money scam."
"You don't have any choice Calypso. It's arranged."
"What the fuck do you mean?"
"Ok here it is, on the line. You, me and Delph are authorised to sign the cheques for the estate until Salvador comes of age at eighteen. That's eight years away. Delph and I will cut your money off if you don't go."
"My aunt wouldn't do that, she likes me."
"That's exactly why she would do it Calypso, she loves you, who doesn't?"
"That can work both ways Michael, I can refuse to sign your cheques and drop a few hints to Aunt Delph about some of your 'hobbies' as it were."
"You need the money to live Calypso, I don't, I can live perfectly well from my legal practice and Delph is financially independent."

Calypso frowned but you couldn't tell. She needed Jolyon to support her but he was gone. She needed Jonny to make her laugh but he was gone. She needed Salvador to look at, to see his father in him but he was at Eton. She felt so alone.

It took so long to get better, heal her body, make her beautiful again. The exclusive 'Bon Secours' hospital soon became a padded cell she bounced impatiently around in. It took two months before they released her.

It was a new shape Range Rover that came to collect her. Dark unobtrusive, almost unnoticeable green. It was the same driver, try as she might she couldn't remember his name. He'd told her a long time ago when she'd been drunk. Now she was sober. He helped her with the two small bags.

"Thank you."

She looked at the small thin man. He was about fifty years old, 'perhaps he was a retired jockey?' She thought to herself.

"What's your name?" The accident could now be used as an excuse for her bad memory.

"Timothy Ma'am. Tim Hogan."

"What did you do before you took this job Tim?"

He looked at her, surprised at her interest.

"Horses Ma'am, ride and train horses."

"Why did you stop?"

"A horse will always find some way to bite you Ma'am and I'm not so fast or bendy as I used to be."

"Safer if the horses are under a bonnet eh Tim."

"Exactly Ma'am." They both laughed.

Luggala looked wonderful. As they crested the small rise, just after the cattle grid, coming out from the high bank of the hill on one side and the line of trees on the other, she couldn't help but take a deep breath in, as though surfacing from a dive. The open pastures surrounding the little white faux castle made you do it. Made you fill your lungs with space and clean green air.

They quietly pulled up on the comforting scrunching fine gravel. Nothing had changed. All the staff were clustered 'round the front doors. She hugged them all. Michael, Delph and Salvador of course couldn't be there. Salvador was due home for Easter soon The helicopter would fetch him.

There was no decanter in her room, 'that was good' she thought to herself. The pain of her injuries had somehow overridden her need to 'wash' her thoughts with alcohol everyday then as the pain and discomfort slowly dissolved she began to feel strong. Stronger than before.

 Calypso stood in front of the tall thin windows of her room and looked out at the familiar view stretching green and distant, till the pastures, trees and sky became one. She'd ring Salvador tonight and tell him she was home. God she felt alone, yet there was no one, all this money, all this luxury, all this and no one she could open her heart to. A knock came at her door, she knew it was Tommy.

"Come in Tommy." Tommy timidly entered his flat cap in his hand.

"Yes Ma'am you wanted something?"

"Tommy I want you to fix my car."

Tommy looked at her as though she'd asked him to turn the rain off.

"It's a bit of a wreck Ma'am."

"I don't care, it started life as a kit car just buy a new chassis and body then transfer all the bits."

"Quite a few of 'the bits' are broken Ma'am it'll be an expensive job."

"I don't care just fix it, it's part of my past, my life when I was young and happy. Just fix it."

"Yes Ma'am."

Tommy left, he was a nice man, a quiet man, but he existed in a lower world, he didn't understand. She couldn't talk to him about important or personal things. She couldn't really talk to anyone in the house except herself. She felt like a drink, in the hospital it was impossible, there were always staff, nurses, doctors fussing about, coming and going but here there was no one, it was definitely possible.

Mothers room was across the gallery, it was always kept locked with the key in the outside lock. Mother had wandered off a couple of times. The first time she'd been found lying in a field of cabbages half frozen to death, the second wandering about in the woods. Police dog 'Ken' knew her scent pretty well and managed to find her before she'd died of exposure.

"Are you a new maid?" Mother enquired haughtily. "If you are, I don't want you, I want the old one. Get out!"

"No, I'm your daughter Calypso. Sit down mother let me sort your clothes out, your dress is back to front."

"Daughter! Daughter! I haven't got a daughter. You're an impostor after money. You won't get any, I don't sign cheques anymore."

The room smelled of piss and shit, it had a large ensuite bathroom but she rarely used it.

"Father Hughes is coming this afternoon. We're going to Lourdes, we go every year you know. What's your name? They keep changing the staff here and I can't keep up with all the names. The nuns look after me very well you know, it's a long way to Lourdes. I love kissing and stroking the stone. You have to queue up for ages to do it. There's always a big queue but father Hughes somehow manages to get me in the front. We're leaving at two so I must get ready."

"I'm Calypso your daughter and you're not going to Lourdes this afternoon."

"Oh aren't I? Have I got the day wrong? Is it tomorrow?" Father Hughes and the nuns are very good to me you know, they always get me to the front of the queue at Lourdes and Father Hughes always gets me some Holy Water. You look just like a man I knew. One of the nuns, Sister Mary I think it was, said she'd never seen my hair looking so beautiful. We're going to Caldey Island next week. I love the Monastery there, I'd stay there but it's just monks, they're really good to me as well, they usually give me some home made lemon curd. The monks really like me you know. One of them said that if he wasn't a monk he'd want to marry me. He was joking of course."

"Stand up mother while I sort your clothes out. What man?"

"A man on a Caribbean Island. Maybe it was a dream? I've never been on a Caribbean Island. I've been to Caldey Island. It has a beautiful church, you can hear the sea inside the church."

"What was the man's name?"

"Ralph, I'm going to Caldey Island next week. Father Hughes is picking me up at six in the morning, we have to go early as it's a long way."

"What island?"

"Martinique, it's French you know. The Captain chose it as being French it would have decent food."

Calypso went over to the drawer for some clean pants. She was apprehensive about opening the drawer. Sure enough, on the right a pile of clean pants had been neatly folded and stacked by the laundry maid but on the left there were two piles with soiled pants hiding them.

There was a shout.

"What are you doing in my drawers? Get out! Get out of my drawer and get out of my room."

"I just have to clean up a bit. I won't be long."

"I knew you were the maid. Pretending to be my daughter. I knew it. I may be old but I'm not stupid. You won't get any money, I don't sign any cheques anymore. I'm going to Lourdes this afternoon. Did I tell you-------------."

Calypso took the plastic bag out of her pocket and quickly put the soiled pants into the bag before quickly leaving. She could hear her mother shouting from the other side. 'Please, if there is a God, don't let me be like that.' Calypso quietly muttered to herself.

God she needed a drink.

Phoning Salvador was 'by appointment' there were no phones in the rooms so he had to walk into town to one of the four phone boxes. It was seven'o'clock on Mondays and Friday nights.

The summons to the hall phone worried her she skipped quickly down the wide marble stairs.

"It's Master Salvador." Said the nervous maid as she handed the phone to Calypso.

"Hello Mother." Salvador's voice sounded nervous, almost timid.

"What's wrong? You never call me."

"Nothing's wrong Mother, It's just that I've been invited by Grandpa Baltimore to stay at Bovington for the Easter break and I wanted to let you know." There was a long silence.

"Did you hear me OK Mother?"

"Yes! Yes! That's fine, you have a lovely time. Maybe I'll fly over for a day just to have a catch up with you."

"No. No, don't do that mother, Grandpa and Grandma have arranged a few things for me, visits, the seaside, that sort of thing so I'm not sure where exactly I'll be." There was another short silence.

"OK, you have a great time and pass on my regards." Calypso didn't wait for an answer. She put the phone down on her son.

Deflated, she glanced over at the maid waiting near the door.

"Take a decanter up to my room, make sure it's good and make sure it's full."
"Yes Ma'am."

Chapter 4

Somehow he just didn't feel safe without Sandra around. Her strength was a comfort to him. Her beauty hidden, locked away inside. He had a key but she had her own life.

The entrance to his partitioned pretend room was just a curtain that slid on a pole. It was elevenish when the curtain was whisked briskly back and Edenson entered.

"Long time no see Mr. Leonard Flower Joel." There was no proffered hand, not even a welcoming smile. Edenson was, as before. Dark blue Saville Row suit, cream shirt and a purple tie with maybe just a hint of pink. Shoes were black leather brogues, hair was neatly cut. His round fat face lifted from a schoolboy photo. He didn't enquire how he was.

"Hello Mr. Edenson, have you come to give me some money?"

Edenson winced and furrowed his brow at his vitriolic directness.

"I'm here to help you Mr. Joel. You know we always look after the welfare of our - ." He paused to think. - "Associates. The images on the ATM cameras were clearly not of you so we stopped your card."

"So, who do you want me to kill this time?"
"Clearly you're not in any position or, dare I say, condition to kill a fly so my visit is purely a welfare one. Special Branch are looking at the people who 'ensnared' you so to speak, so you've no need to worry about them. After you've been discharged from here which will be next Monday, we've arranged a couple of months 'recuperation' for you in a rather exclusive place in the country, just to make sure your little inconvenient habit is got rid of. If you understand me."
"What if I don't want to be 'recuperated'."
"Then you don't get the new card that's in my wallet."
"How much?"
"Three hundred pounds per month."

Joel lay back on the pillows.

"OK I'll go, but after it I want two air tickets to Hong Kong. A little holiday to recover from my 'rehabilitation', sorry 'recuperation'."

Edenson looked at him.

"Don't push it too far Mr. Joel we do have others you know."
"Yes or no?"
"Yes." Edenson hated Joel's directness, he much preferred the unspoken subtlety of high end diplomacy.
"What's the name of this place?"
"Bicknor Court."
"Where is it?"
"In the country. A car will pick you up at nine next Monday morning."

Edenson took out his wallet and gave Joel a plastic bank card. He left without saying goodbye.

It was boring in the hospital, there was a TV but he found the BBC channels stilted and the ITV channels too oppressive with their constant adverts pushing pushing pushing stuff in his face, smoke these fags and you get to shag this beautiful girl with magnificent tits. Ugly fat people weren't allowed on TV. The nurses were friendly but not as friendly as Sandra. They preferred their patients incapacitated in bed rather than walking about chatting to everyone and making obvious 'tents' in the bed. Sandra rang everyday.

Edenson was right. Joel looked through the rain rivers that ran down his window and could see a new blue Rover Two Thousand sat there waiting patiently in the rain. A besuited driver just sitting there in it, probably listening to the radio. Joel wondered if he had a gun. He wondered if they were about to get rid of him, a troublesome heroin addict with secrets to tell. No, they could have just let him die in hospital if that was the case.

He had nothing other than the clothes he was wearing and his new bank card. Perhaps he could persuade the driver to stop somewhere to buy a few clothes.

A popular patient, Joel thought it sounded like the title of a book 'The Popular Patient' by Leanord Flower Joel. Yes that sounded good but for now it was just handshakes and smiles from the people who had cared for him over the last two weeks. In his bag was a bottle of Methadone to control the pangs. One nurse in particular he'd had a lifetime love affair with conducted in a few seconds through their eyes. Her handshake lasted just a fraction longer. Then it was out into the cold grey rain. Not heavy rain but the persistent all drenching rain that never lets up.

He ran over to the blue Rover. On seeing him the driver got out to open the rear door. For an old looking man he moved surprisingly quickly.

"Hello." Joel said as he dived for the back seat,throwing the small bag onto the other side of the seat.

"Good morning Sir." The 'Sir' was a statement of intent that they weren't going to become best chums on the journey.

"Where are we going?"

"Bicknor Court Sir."

"And where exactly is Bicknor Court?"

"Nearly in Wales Sir."

"Can we listen to Radio 1?"

The chauffeur made no comment and pressed the fourth button on the Pye Radio. 'Yesterday' by the Beatles came out of the speakers. It took him back to Happy Valley, his mother's yurt and Welsh wet green rain that somehow seemed different to English rain. The car purred it's way south.

"Can we stop in a town or city on the way? I need to buy some clothes."

"How about Birmingham Sir?"

"Do you know your way around the city centre?"

"Yes Sir, I'd suggest Rackhams for basic good quality clothing."

"Fine. Thank you." Joel sunk back into the leather seat, considered taking a swig from the Methadone bottle but decided against it. 'Gieves' would clock him in the mirror and he'd be marked down a point or two.

"What's this Bicknor Court like?"

"It's a large remote country house Sir. Very peaceful and secluded also very expensive I believe, so you must be of some importance Sir."

Joel laughed. "I'm the least important person you'll ever meet."

"I doubt that Sir."

Gieves parked the car at a parking meter. He didn't put any money in it.

"Rackhams and Beaties are just up that road Sir about a quarter of a mile, you should find something suitable there Sir. I'll wait here."

His constant use of 'Sir' was beginning to irritate Joel "Aren't you coming to get some lunch or something?" He enquired.

"No Sir, I have some sandwiches and a flask here." He wondered who had made the sandwiches and filled the flask. He suspected whoever it was, was trapped in a joyless marriage.

Rackhams came up first. People flitted in and out of the large wooden revolving doors like bees going into a hive. It looked as though it hadn't moved on from the fifties. Before he committed to the middle class whirligig he'd check out the place across the road.

'The Oasis' was a hippy clothes market. A hotchpotch of colour and disorder catering to wandering free minds. Afghan sheepskin coats, tie dye 't' shirts, posters of Jimi Hendrix, Mick Jagger and John Lennon, mini skirts and even shorter 'mini' dresses.

"Sorry man we don't do cards, just cash." The black man with a rainbow coloured tea cozy on his head drawled as Joel tried to buy two pairs of jeans, two floral shirts, one purple, one deep red and a green corduroy jacket.

'Rackhams it is then.' He thought to himself. At least 'Syd Snot' will approve.

They did do jeans in Rackhams but they were very traditionally cut, almost 'workwear'. Shirts, pullovers and jumpers were also 'conservative' but he did find a nice dark blue Duffle coat.

Beaties provided some socks, pants, hankies, an umbrella and a brown leather jacket.

Joel made his way back towards the Rover, he had no cash for a sandwich. The card Edenson had given him was a Barclays card. He'd try it out in a Barclays Bank.

It was like walking into hallowed halls, his brightly coloured, almost cardboard, carrier bags seemed to make twice as much noise. Everyone in there was formal, even the customers.

"Hello. Can I get some money from my card please?"

The teller, behind elegant black cast iron bars, looked him up and down before taking his card. He inspected the card, then looked at Joel again.

"One moment Sir." The teller looked just like you would expect a teller to look. Thin, forty three years old, no hair on the top of his head, thin face to go with his body, frameless glasses with a cord around his neck, a dark suit, light blue shirt with a waistcoat. Joel thought his name would be Edward or maybe James but definitely not 'ed' or 'jim'. Whatever his name was it would have to match his tie. He disappeared into an office with a stout wooden door.

Joel stood there, surrounded by carrier bags feeling like a bank robber more than a bank customer. The room had a very high ceiling from which lights dangled on very long chains.

"This is a Government card Sir."

"Yes I know."

"Do you have any identification?"

"No." there was a long pause as the man studied the card again and then studied Joel.

"How much do you want?"

"Twenty pounds should do." the man turned away for a small hand machine that pressed the embossed details of the card onto a multi layered small form.

"Sign here." Edward slid the form under the bars and gestured towards a biro attached by a plastic spiral to the Bank.

"Thank you." Joel signed and pushed it back. The teller reluctantly passed over four five pound notes. He was worried about his pension, uncomfortable and not at all happy about the transaction.

The five pound note seemed inappropriate at the sandwich bar that sheltered in the entrance to the bus station.

"Sorry, that's all I've got." It took the fat man in the white coat and small white hat an age to sort his change.

He expected 'Syd Snot' to be asleep in the car but he wasn't.

"I'll put your goods in the boot Sir."

Joel noticed a Traffic Warden policing the long row of meters, from his direction he must have passed the Rover, yet there was no ticket despite the red flag of the meter plain to see.

"Traffic Warden not a problem?" Joel asked.

"No. Not a problem Sir." There was an element of 'steel' in his reply. Joel was now more certain he had a gun.

The Rover purred into life.

"I need to get some toiletries if you see a convenient supermarket." He thought of asking his name but decided against it.

"All toiletry requirements will be provided at Bicknor Court."

"Oh!" There was a pause for thought. "That's good. How long before we get there?"

"About two and a half hours Sir."

Joel thought of trying to be discreet with his 'tot' of methadone, gave up on the idea and just did it openly from his bag on the seat beside him. 'Syd' glanced into the second mirror. The first one angled to see through the rear window. The second one, the small one fixed with a rubber suction cup, was angled at him. He glanced into it but said nothing. Fitful sleep came and went with the bumps and traffic.

It was getting towards four o'clock when they veered off the main dual carriageway and headed into a small market town. Joel had missed the name. A large school on the left was discharging it's pupils, running, shouting, laughing, pulling, pushing, thumping, grabbing and touching as only children have the freedom to do. The Rover slowed then halted as a 'yellow' man with a 'lollipop' stop sign walked out to the middle of a 'Zebra' crossing signalling the tide of children to cross. It took three minutes before the man gave in and moved aside.

The road funneled into a narrow street with shops either side then rose up to a wide area with an old stone market house on the right. A Police Officer with large white gloves stood in the middle of the crossroads directing traffic. Joel watched from the back as they queued. It seemed apparent that the officer was giving priority to the more prestigious expensive cars. He probably knew who was in them. Joel thought, then quickly disposed of the notion as preposterous.

The other side of the crossroads was narrow, two cars could just about pass by, lorries and vans had to give way to each other. An old pub on the left seemed to hang slightly over the pavement, the buildings on the right seemed to lean back away from the pavement as though a huge wind was blowing the buildings over. After about five hundred yards the road widened and rose more steeply giving way to a park on the left and a Police Station on the right.

"How much further?" Joel chirped from the back.
"About twenty minutes Sir."

Out of town, round a sharp corner, through a village, across a railway junction, over a river bridge, up a hill, under a stone bridge, turn right into another village, turn right again at the entrance to a castle then up a long windey lane through dark woods across a cattle grid and through open pastures. 'Syd Snot' obviously knew the route well. They came to a large wooden gate, a lane eased itself left then collapsed into an unmetalled track, a small track dived off to the right, a small sign said there was a youth hostel down there, an even smaller sign said there was a church. The Rover slowed then went carefully through the open wooden gate. This lane was immaculate. A metalled smooth surface led off for about half a mile to a pale yellow very large mansion.

"Here we are Sir. Bicknor Court, safe and sound."

The taciturn driver pulled the Rover up in front of the main doors. The entrance was a large semicircle of ancient glass supported in wood and iron. The glass rippled and distorted what remained of the day's light. The floor was large black and white tiles. Three yards inside the stylish porch were the doors. Thick solid wood, painted white. A large brass knob and hand plate complemented the white. People just appeared to carry his bag, his shopping, and to guide him in. Joel looked around but the Rover had gone.

"Good afternoon Sir."

The voice was a man in his fifties, a little overweight with curly brown hair sitting on top of a congenial round face that smiled. It was the sort of package that was hard to dislike and invoked feelings of trust.

"My name is Jonathan, this is Mr. Robert, he will take your bags and search them for anything that we don't like here. Is there anything we should know about?"
"There's a bottle of methadone the hospital gave me."
"What about yourself? Anything concealed in odd places?"
"No, you can look in any odd place you like."
"Thank you Sir, we will."
"Follow me Sir, by the way what would you like to be called?"
"Most people just call me Joel."
"OK Joel it is."

Inside the doors was a round hall with a large white marble staircase leading off upstairs. At various points around the circle were stout wooden white doors and then at the back a passageway that led off somewhere. The light was rapidly disappearing, the glazed dome above the hall gathered in what it could. Jonathan turned on the lights. Elegant wall lights and a large cut glass chandelier immediately transformed the circle into a bright theatre of former magnificence. It was easy to imagine well dressed guests gathering for a dinner, a party or a dance. Some of the walls had light defined blanks where once, large family portraits had hung for many years.

"This way Mr. Joel, come into my office."
"Welcome to Bicknor Court, please sit down, we have a few initial formalities then you can retire to your room and rest. Dinner is between six and seven in the dining room. We expect our residents to be reasonably dressed for that. Nothing formal, just smart casual you understand."
"I haven't got many clothes." Joel looked over the large dark wood desk
"I'm sure you'll manage. Now according to your papers you're currently on twenty milligrams a day of Methadone. Is that correct?"

"Yes."

"Are you--" there was a pause as the two men looked directly at each other. - "supplementing' that with anything?"

"If I've got money and the opportunity of course, who wouldn't? Twenty barely keeps you from rattling."

"What about now?"

"I've taken forty today so I'm OK."

"Have you got anything at all in your possessions or on or in yourself that you shouldn't have?"

All of Jonathan's questions were blunt, direct and precise. They were softened by a smile that disguised them almost to the point of friendly concern

"No."

"The drug tests will hopefully confirm that. You will have two tests everyday, one at nine in the morning and one as you enter the dining room for dinner."

"What if I'm not hungry?"

"We come and knock at your door."

"As you know this is a very exclusive facility funded mainly by her Majesty's Government. We have a few private clients here but not many. They are usually very elite people with transient problems so we ask, or rather require, everyone to sign a confidentiality agreement. Is that OK with you Joel?"

"Yes I suppose so but I'm really not that important."

"You must be of some importance or you wouldn't be here."

"Or of some use?"

"Precisely."

"So what do I do here?"

"You're here Joel to get off heroin, now to help you we have a lot of things to fill your time, tomorrow you'll be shown around. At the rear of this house is a large complex offering almost every interest you can think of, from messing around with old cars to gardening, pigs and chickens. We like to think we have something for everyone and of course we have extensive grounds you can walk around and relax in."

"What if I walk too far?"

"The tag on your ankle will tell us that you need guidance as it were."

"What if I don't want to have a tag on me."

"Then we say goodbye. Kevin will take you to the nearest bus station with enough money to buy a ticket and that's it."

"Is that his name? Wondered what it was? What about my card?"

"That wouldn't work I'm afraid, I'm sure we won't have such problems Joel. You look such an intelligent young man. Now I'll get someone to show you to your room, relax, have a bath, listen to the radio til sixish then come down for dinner, you'll find the food very good, then tomorrow you can explore and get to know the place. It has a lot of history. You'll enjoy it, many of our guests don't want to leave." Jonathan pressed a buzzer on his desk and within seconds there was a courteous quiet knock on the door and a man in his fifties appeared.

"Ah! Geoffrey, this is Mr. Joel, take him upstairs to the Kings Room will you?"

"Follow me young man." Geoffrey said.

Joel followed the man who walked with difficulty and used his hand to almost pull himself up the bannister stair rail. By the time they reached the top the man was out of breath.

"You're a very lucky young man you know." He croaked. "This place is the best, if you don't get off it here you never will and you'll be dead before long."

"Well that's a cheerful thought." Joel responded.

The King's room was large with three large windows that in the daylight gave magnificent views over pastures and forests but for now the long heavy brocade curtains were drawn over the night blackness.

"Why's it called the King's Room?"

"Cause a king lived in it when he was a baby and up to the age of eight."

"Which king?"

"Edward the fifth."

"Are there any ghosts?"

"No."

"What do you do here?"

"General dog's body, spent most of my life in and out of nick cause of gear. Then Mr Jonathan saved me."

"Thought this was some sort of government place?"

"It is but Mr. Jonathan likes to help out people as well."

"Who owns it?"

"Mr. Jonathan's family, their staunch Catholics, the estate has been in the family for centuries, there's no shortage of money."

"What's your name again?"

"Geoffrey with a 'g' not a 'j' and it's never 'geof'." Joel put out his hand. It was taken by Geoffrey.

"Don't fuck it up here young man, it's the best chance you'll ever get."

"I'm here for a reason Geoffrey, no idea what it is but I'll guarantee it isn't nice."

"Dinner in thirty minutes, I'll show you around the place tomorrow if you'd like."

"Thank you. I'd like that." Geoffrey left, Joel shut the heavy wood door and looked around. It was a huge room, 'big enough for a king' he thought to himself. Next to the table were all his bags and shopping. A large, threadbare in places, carpet looked small on the polished wood floor. On the right hand end of the room was an obviously false partition hiding a bathroom and toilet, a shower with a huge shower head lurked over the large cast iron bath. The bed was large and made of oak, there were two large cast iron radiators. Joel knew they would struggle to warm such a large room when it really got cold. He sat on the bed and unpacked his new clothes. They weren't exactly his taste but then again Rackhams wasn't really his type of shop. Lying down the silence overtook him. It was absolute, the hospital was reasonably quiet but there was always something going on. This was silent

The silence and the energy expended on the day combined to take him into irresistible sleep. Then there was a strong knocking on the door. Joel stirred and looked at the big round clock on the far wall. Twenty past six. Jonathan was right, they did knock on your door.

The knocker was tall and thin with blonde short hair.

"Hi, my name's Trevor, I'm one of the male nurses, dinners being served, oxtail stew or baked cod in a mild cheese sauce tonight but before you go down, need to take a mouth swab and a couple of your hairs for the lab."

Joel opened his mouth wide whilst Trevor brushed the inside of his cheek. Then a quick snip with some surgical scissors.

"What do they need the hair for?"
"Shows long term drug use."
"What do you reccomend?"
"The oxtail stew, it's delicious, apple crumble and custard afterwards. The chef's ex Navy, looks awful, tastes delicious."

There were about twenty people of all types in the large room. He was the new kid on the block so everyone looked at him for a second before the hum of eating resumed. A hatch on the right gave access to a chef clad in white and blue with a huge kitchen behind him.

"What's it to be young man?"

Joel looked at the chalkboard on the easel to the right. There were two choices as Trevor had said.

"Oxtail please."
"And?"
"Rhubarb crumble please."
"Apples are our own, they're in season, rhubarbs out of a tin."
"Rhubarb please."
"With custard or plain yogurt?"
"Custard please."

"OK coming up, drinks are on the top table over there, take a seat I'll shout when it's here. What's your name?"

"Joel."

The chef was about forty, quite fat with a beard. The white chefs hat that towered on his head made him look taller than he was. He looked as though he could be a 'granddad' even if he wasn't. There were about ten round tables in the room. The room was pleasantly warm and smelt of food. It's large tall windows were blocked out by long blue thick velour curtains, the lighting was two elegant chandeliers. Joel guessed at some time it had been a ballroom full of dancing gay people. He moved towards the drinks table. Orange juice, tea, coffee, water and milk were available. He chose some orange juice and turned around.

Three tables had two people at each, two tables had three people, one table had four people and three tables just had one person at each. He paused waiting for a sign.

"Mind if I sit here?"

The sole occupant of the table was thin.

"Not at all, please sit down." The voice was cultured, almost 'effete',
Before sitting Joel offered his hand.
"My name's Joel." His hand wasn't accepted.
"Sorry, I don't like touching people. I'm haphephobic, it's not you it's me. My name's Constantine, most people call me Con, or Connie."

"Oxtail for Mr. Joel." The voice rang out from behind the hatch. Joel walked over to collect a large Royal Worcester china plate with oxtail stew, carrots, broccoli, four roast potatoes and a matching bowl with rhubarb crumble hiding under a generous amount of custard.

"Two months here and you'll be fat." Constantine remarked.
Joel could see the remains of salad on his plate.
"You may be right, I'm not used to good food."
Constantine looked at Joel.
"No, I can see that. Heroin?"
Joel's eyes looked into Constantine's eyes searching for trust, he found a very deep pool of it in the left hand corner.
"Yes. You?"
"No, maybe I'll tell you one day if we become friends"
"I think we're already friends." Joel said, picking up his knife and fork.

"It'll need salt and pepper, the chef never puts enough in." Constantine remarked.

Joel looked around the large room, there were six large oil portraits of regal looking old men. From the clothes, they were obviously from different generations, different times, from the large, sometimes hooked noses they were obviously the same family. They were all men. There were three places that had once held similar pictures but now all that remained was a difference in the shade of paint on the wall.

"Who are the men?" Joel asked.
"Members and descendants of the Vaillancourt family, originally French of course."

The oxtail was delicious, so was the crumble.

"Do you have a TV in your room?" Joel asked.
"No, no one does. There's a TV lounge though."
"Where is it?"
"Next door to Mr. Jonathan's office but to be honest I find the current offerings more in tune with Daily Mirror of Sketch readers than Oxbridge folk."
"Are you an Oxbridge person?"
"Cambridge fifty nine to sixty two."
"What did you learn?"
"How to get a good job without really trying." A shadow of a smile scurried for a second over his thin lips. Everything about Constantine Ellis was thin, especially his shadow. "No, I did the Classics, specialised in North Africa and Turkey. I'm a bit of a 'fringe' person."
"What was the 'good' job?"
Constantine looked at Joel as he took a sip of orange juice.
"Assistant to the Assistant to the Assistant of the Cultural Attache at the Istanbul Embassy."
"A spy then?"
There was another look, another pause as Constantine pondered.
"Yes."
"How come you're here then?"
It was too direct, too sudden, too soon in their friendship.
"I'm having another orange juice, Would you like one?"
"Yes please."

Joel noticed that his blue cord trousers fitted at his small waist but his legs seemed spindly inside the fabric, as though there were no legs there. For a young man his walk was awkward.

"Are we allowed to use a phone?" Usually in these places there's a public payphone, he thought to himself. Most of the time people would be queueing up to use it but here there was nothing. It made him think of the scruffy red public payphone with it's 'jammed permanently open with a piece of wood', - door at ' Happy Valley' and then his mum and then Janey and then Sandra.

"We're allowed to use the one in Jonathan's office but he's obviously there so can hear what you're saying."

"That's not very private."

"It's that or write a letter. I prefer a letter myself. The stamps are free. Jonathan puts them on for you so that he can see who you're writing to."

"Sounds like a prison."

"It's not, you can always walk out but if you do, you can't come back and if the government is supporting you that stops. I'm OK I've got private means."

"How long have you been here?"

"Six weeks."

"How much longer have you got?"

There was another impasse in their conversation.

"As long as I need, til I decide to move on, feeling better."

"Oh.----- Are you going to watch TV?' Joel asked.

"No, I'm tired, I'm going to lie on my bed and think."

"What about?"

"If you like I'll show you around tomorrow morning."

"I'd like that. Geoffrey said he would but I'll cancel him and tag along with you if that's OK?"

"OK, see you at breakfast." Constantine wiped his lips with the serviette and placed it neatly on the side plate. As he stood up a woman in what looked like nuns clothing appeared and whisked his place setting away.Joel watched him walk towards the door, he had that sort of lank but gentle wavy brown hair that only public schoolboys have. The sort of hair that would even look good in a communal boys shower or a Mess ceremonial dinner. There was a sadness about Constantine as though there was something missing in his life.

He knocked on Mr. Jonathan's door.

"May I use the phone?"

"Yes of course, use the extension on the desk by the window."

Joel checked his small notebook, he could never remember her number.

"Hello Sandra -----------."

Chapter 5.

'What's it all about when you sort it out Alfie?
Are we meant to take more than we give?

Only fools are kind--- Alfie.'

Cilla Black warbled out of her radio. Calypso poured another large shot of 'Irish' into the heavy square cut glass tumbler

If she did her hair and put on some make up she still looked good but the girl's body had left her long ago. Now she hated the size of clothes she wore. Now she was a middle aged woman who no one really wanted. Looking through the window and with the help of some whisky she'd change everything tomorrow. Go out, get a job, anything but not this nothing. The Clays were stealing her beloved Salvador. Michael O'Brien and Aunt Delph had instructed the staff to keep her quiet and happy with as much decent whisky as she needed. She wanted for nothing but had nothing.

She knew there was something brewing when Michael and Delph turned up in the afternoon at the same time. They never did that. They didn't even like each other but both played their parts, both took as much money as they possibly could before Salvador took over when he was eighteen. There was a knock at her door.

"We're worried about you Calypso. Concerned about your health." Michael said.

"Shit! You're worried I might sober up and start looking at your expenses, might tell Salvador what aresholes you both are, tell him not to give you a penny once he's eighteen."

"Now there's no need for that sort of language, our roles and thus our remuneration are quite clearly laid out in our contracts so nothing you can do can affect that."

"You drafted out the bloody contracts Michael, bet If I got an independent solicitor to look at then they'd say they were so favourable to you both that they smacked of corruption."

"As Michael said Calypso we're seriously concerned about your health, so much so we'd like you to go to the very discreet comfortable place we know for some help." Aunt Delph was in her late fifties and had married the Captain's brother in the thirties after a whirlwind romance in Cannes. He'd been killed in the war, she'd never remarried or even looked. She didn't really like men, considered them simple and crude.

"What if I don't go, what if I don't want to go?"

"We'll make a formal application to take over your obligations in the running of the estate on the grounds of diminished responsibility due to alcoholism."

Calypso stared at them both. She could tell they weren't bluffing.

"We've got statements from the staff as to your consumption of whisky and behaviour." Michael chipped in.

"What bloody behaviour, I don't do anything."

"You took out your car and crashed it."

"That wasn't my fault, you know that."

"Nevertheless we had to fake your medical condition to stall the police from taking a blood sample."

Calypso deflated into a chair.

"And afterwards, when I'm better, what then?"

"We buy you a modest residence at a location of your choice but not here at Luggala and give you an allowance, enough to live comfortably and you'll have your independence."

"In other words you're kicking me out."

"We see it as being cruel to be kind Calypso, you'll drink yourself to death here and neither myself or your aunt want that. When Salvador comes of age, and that's only eight years away, things will change, we will step back and you will assume whatever role you and Salvador agree to."

Calypso stared out of the window, she wasn't one of them, she was the product of glorious indiscretion. It had taken until she was at least thirty to realise it.

"When do you want me to go?"

Michael O'Brien permitted himself a very fleeting smile as he glanced at Delph.

"The helicopter will take you there tomorrow morning, weather permitting. It's for the best, you know that. Jolyon wouldn't want you this way."

Calypso turned to face him with such speed it made him back away.

"Jolyon never wanted me anyway. It was a convenient marriage of families, you know that." She spat out the words. "I did love him, he was my childhood playmate but not my soulmate. Jonny Conrad was my soulmate and my lover. I'm sure that little fucking midget Hetty Betts caused the death of both of them. I'm sure in my heart and my head but nobody will take notice of either."

"You're talking nonsense Calypso, Jolyon's was a tragic accident and Jonny Conrad came from a working class background, couldn't cope and took the easy way out. You know that."

"Jonny Conrad never took the easy route to anywhere. He didn't have to. He was the best." Calypso paused and stared again out of the window. "At everything." There was another pause. " I don't want Salvador to know, tell him I've gone on a trip to the Caribbean to search for my father."

"We can't do that." Delph brusquely retorted. "We don't want him to know that he's got."

Calypso sliced into her words.

"Got what? Aunt Delph. A Black ancestor, a negro grandfather, a poor relative?"

"Mixed genes is the term I would prefer."

Calypso disengaged, it was a battle she'd never win.

It was her last night at Luggala for a while, maybe forever, she thought, swirling the whisky around the bottom of the glass before emptying it. The glass was empty, so was the decanter. It was one in the morning the helicopter was scheduled for nine. She never made it into her bed, just onto it. She rolled over and stared at the ceiling, it was plain white, here was no wonderful painting that made you marvel, no young body that made you gasp with pleasure, no hard unstoppable urgency that spilled out satisfaction. If only he'd made her pregnant, if only she'd had his child, everything would have been so different. Sleep came but it was to be of no value. She'd wake up tired.

The knocking started faintly and became louder as her impaired senses woke up.
"Yes Yes! I'm awake."
"The man said the helicopter is scheduled to take off in an hour Ma'am. The man said he can't be late because of the flight plan and the clearances Ma'am."

The voice behind the door was young, small and female. It was the new maid. They had told Calypso her name but she couldn't remember it. These days she could only remember someone's name on the second attempt.

"Yes. Yes. I'll be there, are my bags ready to go?"
"Yes Ma'am."

Calypso dashed to the garage with Tommy. The little dark green Lotus Elan looked shiny and eager with it's new body and parts. Tommy had done a good job rebuilding it. Calypso ran her hand along it and grasped the wood of the steering wheel.

"Look after it for me Tommy. It's got a lot of happy memories for me."
"Don't you worry Ma'am, it'll be here waiting for you when you get back."

She looked at him.

"Do you think I'll make it back Tommy?"
"You've got a son Ma'am, at the moment he's learning about people and life but eventually he'll come back home and bring his 'mum' with him."
"If I don't make it Tommy, make sure he gets my car will you."
"Don't you be thinking like that! Life can be full of surprises."

Calypso leant forward and kissed him on the cheek.

"Got to fly."

Chapter 6.

"Fancy a walk, I've discovered a secret place." Constantine placed the two cups of coffee down on the table.

"I'm not feeling too good this morning Connie. They reduced me to twelve mill yesterday."

"That's good isn't it? Only three weeks ago you were on twenty. Come on, the fresh air will do you good."

"Yes and no, I feel shit, every bone in my body aches. I want to pull them out and give them a good scratch."

"Well don't, you'll make an awful mess." They both laughed. Connie more exuberantly than Joel.

It was a beautiful November morning. The white light of the winter sun was chasing the morning white frost from the sloping pasture as it moved across. Nothing escaped it's caress. Constantine wore blue cord trousers, a sleeved vest covered by a check shirt, partially covered by a brown pullover, a short dark green Barbour jacket, a burberry scarf but no hat.

They used the back entrance, a stout varnished door now fitted with a keypad entry system plus a silver button you pressed if you were a stranger or had forgotten the code. Jonathan always answered. The door led out into a very large tarmacked square. A modern accommodation block on the right, access to the front of the house to the left, then a row of garages and workshops along the left hand side of the square. At the back of the square was the Vaillancourt family church. Catholic of course and access to the gardens.

"Wow! Look at that!"

"Look at what?" Constantine replied.

"That, over there, you don't see many of those these days, I wonder whose it is?"

"What are you talking about?"

"That dark Green Bristol 400."

"It's mine." Constantine added.

Joel stopped in his tracks and looked at his friend up and down.

"That figures!" They both smiled. Joel put his arm around Constantines shoulder. He didn't think about it. He just did it. Constantine didn't think about it either.

"What's this secret place?"

"Follow me."

"How long for, five minutes, half an hour or the rest of my life?"

The two men stopped in the wan winter morning sun and looked at each other.

"The rest of your life." The moment was broken by laughter leaving an abyss between suggestion and doubt.

They turned left at the church and walked out onto a rock and dirt track that then dropped right behind the church. The track was uneven, unkempt and rutted by rain. It was a track for feet or tractors but nothing in between.

The track eventually led down to the river. The river was almost a moat, encircling the huge mansion topped mound on three sides. The metalled road was the only escape unless you wanted a very cold dangerous swim. There was rumour of a secret passageway that went deep under the river to the village on the other side but if it was true it was a heavily guarded secret. An escape route, should they need it for the Catholic Vaillancourts during the Cromwellian Civil War.

Just past the buildings, on the left was a small copse that rose up, a small, almost invisible track led off through it.

"This way." Constantine pushed aside overhanging brambles laden with blackberries. The tiny path was just uneven brown earth. They struggled along it for about a hundred yards. The path suddenly became stone steps that led down to a place. It was almost magical. There was a spirituality that could almost be touched. The brown earth gave way to a rock 'dent' in the hillside, not a cave but a concave depression in the rock. As though scraped out by a giant with a spoon. The floor had been tiled but dead beautiful leaves added to their decoration, there was an altar made of painted concrete, to the right was a statue of the Virgin Mary looking benevolent in faded falling off paint. To the left was an old wooden bench that looked out down the pastures to the river. It was a place of secret peace, where you had no choice but to internally examine your place in the world. Constantine dropped to his knees in front of the altar, his hands clasped, his eyes closed. Joel just looked at his new friend. After a few moments he got up.

"What do you think? Beautiful isn't it?"
"Are you a Catholic Constantine?"
"I might be, I don't know. I don't know what I am Joel."

Joel sat down on the bench and took in the view. There were cattle, black and white cows, slowly grazing the sloping meadow, finishing off the year's nutrition before they were locked away for the winter. After a few moments Constantine joined him. He sat close to Joel. Their clothes touched. He reached over and gently picked up Joel's hand, clasping it as if in a handshake.

"Actually, that feels quite nice. That's the first time I've touched human flesh since--------- ." Constantine stopped in mid flow.

"Since what? Since when?" He asked.

"Since a long time ago. You like my old Bristol then?"

It was a very definite change of subject, a shutting down.

"Yes it's lovely and very much you."

They sat in silence looking at the pastoral picture that spread out before them.

"How did you happen to become a heroin addict Joel?" Constantine asked, still looking at the view.

"I was in prison, had a lot of stressful things going on in my life, someone suggested I try 'a dig' to relax me and that was it."

"What were you in prison for?"

"Murder."

"That doesn't sound like you, you seem a gentle boy, a country boy."

"I am, and it wasn't like me. I was forced to do it."

"What do you mean? Who by?"

"The government. It's a very long story."

"Well we're not going anywhere." Joel turned and looked at the young fragile man sitting next to him.

"You can hold my hand whilst I tell you the story if you want." Constantine took his hand without looking.

"My mother was a penniless youngster living with her mom and dad in almost poverty. She got into some kind of trouble then had some kind of mental breakdown, they offered her a way out and some regular money if she agreed to be artificially inseminated and had a baby on their terms."

"Who are 'they'?"

"The government, the secret service, whatever you want to call them, anyway the baby was me, no birth certificate, no regular doctors, dentists, schools, nothing, nothing was normal. By this time mum was living in a yurt in a hippy commune in Wales. Looking back I had an incredibly happy childhood, discovering nature, music, people used to turn up two or three times a week to teach me. I thought it was normal. Anyway that all stopped one day when I was summoned to London and very firmly put in the picture. They said I was totally expendable and if I didn't do their bidding I would be - got rid of- they said that there was a poisonous capsule in my jaw that if broken by any kind of blow it would kill me. That turned out to be true but as a result of a bad tooth in Malaya I got rid of it. They put me in the Navy with instructions to get rid of a certain chap, they gave me the means to do it. It was easy. As it turned out - no I won't bore you anymore - suffice to say there was a witness to me doing it. He became a drunk after being demobbed but eventually somebody in the Police believed his story and I got arrested and sent to prison. After about nine months inside they sprung me out to do another job for them but by then i was addicted.

"So how come you're here, this is a very expensive place?"

"After I did the second job for them my mother died and Janey, my partner, got killed in a road accident. I went down hill and got conned by some Animal Libers, they took my government debit card and stole my money, I went up to Newcastle to stay with an old prison mate. I OD'd on gear and blacked out, thought I was dead. This girl I'd met in Kathmandu on the second job, Sandra, saved me. I ended up in hospital then Edenson, the chap who runs me in the secret service, came to the hospital, said they had another job for me but would need me to be clean first so here I am."

Constantine squoze his hand but didn't let go.

"That's quite a tale."

"There's more but it's nasty."

"What about your father?"

"As I said, there's more. Do you think there's anything in this 'religion' thing?" Joel asked, still peering at the vista.

"Not sure, my family are Church of England but it wasn't a big thing in my childhood, when you get older you do consider things don't you?"

"Such as?"

"Well Easter for instance, if you've got the power to come back from the dead why take three days to do it? And why only appear twice?"

"Don't know but it's quite intriguing isn't it. Shall we wander back for lunch, I've got a talking therapy this afternoon."

"Oh dear, poor you, still there's steak and kidney pie for lunch followed by rice pudding or Bakewell tart. Come on."

Joel and Constantine held hands as they walked back through the wood, as they approached the buildings Joel let go.

Chapter 7.

The green helicopter clattered and clawed it's way into the sky before angling over and leaving Luggala behind. Calypso looked back at it and wondered. Wondered if she'd ever see the gilded cage of Luggala again. Wondered where she was going to. There was just the pilot, a navigator, Michael O'Brien and her. She felt so shit from the melancholy ride on the back of whisky last night that conversation was just too much of an effort. Michael was probably quite relieved that was the case. He sat, strapped into the seat in front of her. Helicopters were fast and convenient but shook you like a jelly, the rotors battering her ears. Looking out of the window the browns and purples of the Wicklow mountains sloped gently into the grey blamange of the Irish sea. She could see a ribbon of a road threading it's way through the hills and wondered if it was the road she'd crashed on. Why did that have to happen to her? 'Why me?' She thought then followed it up with 'Why not me?' it was just an unfortunate accident, she was OK her little car was now better than new. What was the problem? Then there were boats, looking like toys in a bath, leaving little trails of bubbles behind them God she could do with a drink!

It took less than forty minutes before they were over land again. Somehow she felt relieved, 'crashing on the land was much less dangerous than crashing into the sea', she thought to herself, then corrected her thoughts 'crashing anywhere was deadly dangerous'. It took another twenty minutes to cross Wales then she could sense the helicopter slowing and descending. Michael strained in his straps to turn round.

"Well here we are Calypso, your new home for a while."

Calypso looked down to see a large hoop of a black river lassoing an isthmus of land with a large yellow house sat on top of a hill.

"Bicknor Court, just in England, remote, peaceful, and expensive so make the most of your stay here Calypso, the estate couldn't sanction a second bite of the cherry as it were."

Calypso got the feeling that for Michael O'Brien and Aunt Delph, paying out for expensive treatment was eminently preferable to having a whisky soaked matriarch around. The helicopter reluctantly settled onto it's wheels in front of the pale yellow house. Calypso looked out of the window, a few people were gathered around the big semicircular front. It almost looked like a Gazebo plonked in front of the doors but it wasn't, its stoutness and firmness marked it down as an original feature. Michael unstrapped himself and opened the side door. The rotors were now lazily swishing around until they stopped altogether. The pilot and navigator climbed down from their perches for a comfort break and a cup of tea.

"Hello." It was a comforting 'hello' with a gap after it, allowing Calypso to look at him. "My name's Jonathan, I'm the manager here, welcome to Bicknor, let me take your bags." His voice was soft, he looked 'soft', tubby but not fat, a round face and unruly brown hair. She'd expected someone more austere, more clinical, perhaps a white coat, maybe a woman doctor with a white coat, hair tied up and tortoise shell glasses. Mr. Jonathan was more in line with a corner shop keeper.

The helicopter had aroused some interest, there were about ten or twelve people now hanging about looking. Calypso handed her small travel bag to him as he held her arm to assist down out of the helicopter. His hand on her arm felt so safe. Everybody walked towards the front door. There was nothing to distinguish it from a home.

Joel and Constantine had just returned from a walk along the river as the green helicopter 'chattered' it's way to land in front of the mellow mansion. There was a large semicircle of tarmac in front of the house. Large enough to wheel your horse and carriage around so it easily coped with a green helicopter.

"Crickey!" Constantine said. "I wonder who's in that?" They both stood in front of the line of trees to the right of the house.
"Probably someone from the government on some sort of inspection."
"Well it doesn't look very military and a woman got out of it, she was quite pretty, a nice tan with dark ringlets for hair, a little plump but still a nice figure. Didn't you see her?"
"Yes, as you say, quite pretty." Joel replied, his eyes somehow riveted to the woman who had delicately descended from the helicopter and was walking towards the front door "Shall we go in, I'm getting cold now we've stopped walking?"
"OK, time for your medicine anyway, what you down to now?"
"Ten but I'm really struggling with it. It's OK if I'm doing something."
"Come on, let's go and play table tennis?"
"No, I don't want to do that." Joel snapped.
"What do you want to do?" Constantine snapped back.
"I don't know! I don't fucking know! I don't even know who I am or what the fuck I'm doing with my life." Joel thumped a tree with his fist.

Constantine stood back and looked at his friend.

"We're all the same here Joel. All lost souls, some being renovated for a reason, some being repaired and some who just can't cope with the things that their money can buy. Whoever you are, whatever you do, I'm here for you, you know that Joel don't you?"

Tears flowed down Joel's cheeks as he turned towards the tree, then back towards Constantine.

"I killed my half brother Connie, killed my half brother and I didn't even know it at the time. You couldn't make it up could you?" Joel collapsed into the tall thin frame and arms of Constantine Ellis sobbing into his pullover. After seconds he pulled away.

"Sorry about that. Let's go in."

The welcoming committee for the dusky lady had disappeared into Jonathan's office.

"What do you think her name is Connie? Arriving in a helicopter, remnants of extreme beauty, it has to be something extraordinary."

"Now you're wrong there young Joel. The 'aristos' usually give their heirs normal names; it's considered 'not good form' to choose unusual names. I'm going for Cecilia."

"Oh no, that just doesn't fit with her presence. I'm going for something with an 'X' in, Oxana."

"There's no such name, you've made it up."

"No I haven't. Here's the bet, when we find out her name we compare it to ours, the one with the most comparable letters wins."

"Ok, you're on. Wins what?" Constantine asked.

"How about we get permission to walk out, go down to the Post Office in the village and the loser buys two bounty bars."

"Why Bounty Bars?"

"Well they sort of go with her, I'm guessing there's a bit of negro blood in her."

"Come on, coffee time." Connie and Joel headed for the kitchen, it was always warm in there.

"What's 'Aristos' mean?" Joel asked.

"Old money, aristocratic. It's Latin."

"It would be." Mumbled Joel. "Let's invite her to our table at dinner, if she comes down."

"Yes Let's." A nun silently made them two cups of coffee, dressed in a fawn habit with a white scapula she moved graciously around the working kitchen, checking this, regulating that, almost effortlessly producing delicious food. It made Joel think of the miraculous feeding of the five thousand by Jesus.

"Do you believe in miracles Connie?"

"Where on earth did that come from?"

"Just thinking that's all, the nun cooking here in the kitchen reminded me of the loaves and fishes miracle."

"You're moving into deep water there my beautiful friend. You'll be wanting to go to church next."

"We've never looked in the church here have we? We could do that tomorrow and there's a church somewhere down by the river, we could have a look at that too."

"What about the Bounty Bars?"

Joel laughed.

"Yes you're right, they're more important than looking in churches. I'm going to my room for a rest before dinner. See you about twelve fifteen."

"Lunch, it's lunch, I'll come with you."

"What, to my room?"

"Yes if you don't mind. I don't want to be alone at the moment." There was a long understanding look between Joel and Constantine Ellis.

"No I don't mind, let's go."

The bed in the King's room was very big, Joel lay down on the right, Constantine on the left, after a while they held hands, after a while they fell asleep.

"Well she's not come to lunch." Connie moved his empty dish formerly known as blueberry pie and custard to one side then placed his napkin on the table in the vacant place.

"Probably resting in her room." Joel replied, sipping at an orange juice. " What shall we do this afternoon?"

"Nothing, I'm going to hospital for a check up."

Joel's eyebrows rose in an unspoken question.

"I got raped." - There was a long pause. - Badly, by a lot of soldiers, had to have some surgery in a painful place."

"Oh! I don't know what to say."

"Then don't say anything, just be there for me at bad moments."

Joel reached out his hand to stroke Connie's hand.

"OK." Joel wanted to ask more but didn't. Connie wanted to talk about it but couldn't.

"What hospital?"

"The Priory, it's a private hospital in Edgbaston Birmingham, Kevin will be my chauffeur so I'm in for a rather quiet journey."

"Yeh! Kevin doesn't really specialise in 'sparkling' conversation does he?" Joel laughed. After a few seconds Connie laughed too.

Joel mooched about all afternoon, it was worse when he had nothing to do, Ros, his therapist wasn't available that afternoon, he hadn't realised how dependent he'd become on Connie's presence and friendship. He couldn't settle into a book, the radio was monotonous, feel good 'Pap' or serious folk just talking, the TV room was always chilly. He lay back on the empty bed and thought about Mum, Janey, Sandra Lenny Welham, horrible Edenson, Bugis Street Singapore, Saul Molloy, Kathmandu, Shivili, the Continental Hotel Saigon, Phu Quoc Island, his dad. He wondered if Connie would be back in time for dinner. He decided to go down and try to ring Sandra.

"Hello you, How's it going?"
"Wow! Hang on, let me put a red ring on the calendar! What's the problem?"
"I've been lying on a bed holding hands with a man."
"So?"
"It didn't bother me. In fact it felt quite comforting."
"Why's he there?"
"Not sure, but I think it's psychological, he's disclosed to me that he was raped, apparently by some soldiers and that it required some kind of surgery, that's literally all he's said."
"How are you doing?"
"I'm down to ten but struggling, I feel shit most days."
"As I read it then you're both damaged people who need each other as support."
"Do you have to be so sensible?"
"As far as you're concerned, yes, as for myself never, should have finished with you when we split at the airport, how can you love a bloke who's never shagged you and probably never will?"
"Same as you can love a practical reliable woman who saved your life and you should really marry but probably never will."
"Let me know when you get desperate?"
"Desperate for what?"
"A shag, marriage or both, they usually go together."
"For gods sake Sandra, get somebody normal, you don't need me dragging you down."
"I do. I need a pretty boy around me to boost my confidence."
"Is that all I am then a glamorous prop?"
"Yes, farm animals and pets aren't all that sexy so I need you."
"I've got a little surprise for you when they let me out of here."
"What is it? A large diamond engagement ring from Tiffany's in New York?"
"No, it's better than that."
"Oh go on tell me then."

"No, it's a surprise, you'll have to wait."

"You're such a shit Joel, can I visit you in that place?"

"No, they don't allow visitors, they interfere with the therapy programmes."

"Oh OK, got to go now honeybunch, got to go and stick my hand into a cows arse. Are you sure you want to marry me?"

"Yes of course, where else would I find a woman with a cow on her arm?"

"There all over the place - Bye, Bye, you take care."

"Bye."

Joel glanced at Jonathan as he left the office.

"She's a vet."

Joel lay on his bed listening for a car and looking for lights. It was dark and he wasn't back yet. Trevor came round as usual for his evening swab. Joel went down to dinner. He sat down alone at their usual table after ordering Shepherds pie and collecting an orange juice. There were about a dozen people in the room, he knew most of their names by now but that was as far as it went. Constantine was his companion.

Then she came in. Black women were usually of no interest but she was fascinating. She dressed to make the most of her shape, hiding the inevitable changes of time and displaying what was left. As she cautiously entered he stood up.

"Hello, would you like to join me?"

She stopped and looked at him.

"I'm a little unsure of what to do, so yes thank you."

He pulled out a chair for her to sit. Her voice was pure velvet, a chocolate fountain that cascaded over him. It started with expensive black high heels, black stockings or tights, he couldn't tell which, a beautifully fitted tight black skirt that finished an inch above her knees, a dark purple soft blouse with sequins, a tiny gold necklace and then her hair, dark, dark ringlets hanging from her head like silk coils of a spring that jingled and jangled with every movement, every nuance of her face and head.

"Hi, my name's Joel, pleased to meet you." He offered her his hand, she took it.

"Hello, my name's Calypso."

"One moment." Joel took out his pen and a paper serviette.

Calypso, Cecilia, Oxana.

"What on earth are you doing?"

"Well, my friend and I watched you arrive from the line of trees to the right of the road, we wondered what your name was, Constantine said that you were very rich and so would have a traditional name like 'Cecilia'. I said that you were far too exotic for anything so boring and opted for 'Oxana'. The bet was that whoever had the most corresponding letters when we found out your name would win a Bounty Bar from the Post Office down in the village. However we both have two letters so that's no good."

"How about I buy you both a Bounty Bar seeing as I'm so rich?"

They both laughed, the darkness of her skin showcased the whiteness of her teeth as her face lit up.

"Now, how do I get some food?"

"Oh! Sorry, you go over to the hatch over there, choose from the two choices that are on the chalkboard, tell the chef what you want and what your name is then go over there to get yourself a drink, come back here and wait till he calls out your name."

"What would you advise?"

"Well I'm having Shepherd's pie, but the Liver and Onions is delicious."

Calypso got up and walked over to the hatch, Joel watched her walk, God she must have been a Goddess a few years ago, even now her bottom sashayed across the room. She knew just how to hold herself, knew how to walk in high heels, knew how to make everyone look at her and they did.

The question he wanted to ask but didn't was - why are you here? Calypso had no such qualms, her looks gave her strength with strangers, it was only when they became friends and knew things about her she became weak.

"Why are you here Joel?"

"Heroin, gear, I'm down to ten mill a day at the moment."

"Ten mill? What does that mean?"

Joel looked quizzically at her, she'd obviously led a very protected life.

"Ten millilitres of Methadone, it's a prescribed Heroin substitute. I was on twenty when I came here a month ago."

"Oh!" - 'Calypso, liver and onions', the unseen voice shouted as the china plate was pushed out.

"Guess that's me."

"Guess it is, can't see anybody else in this room who could carry off the name 'Calypso' with such panache and style."

"Are you always such a flatterer."

"No, I'm very picky."

Joel and Calypso looked at each other with the lingering eyes of attraction. Soon she was back, even carrying a hot plate she moved her body to a place called desire. She didn't sit, more curved herself onto the seat.

"Apparently this is a very discreet expensive place Joel. Are you rich?"

"No, I have nothing."

"Then who's paying?"

"The government."

"You must be special."

"More useful, definitely not special."

"You look pretty special to me."

Their eyes lingered just a fraction longer than was necessary before they both laughed. Then some lights flashed across the windows.

"That will probably be Constantine, he's been to hospital today, please excuse me whilst I make sure he's OK."

Joel rose from the table.

"Is he special?" Calypso jumped way into the future of their lives.

He looked at her.

"Very special, if he's up to it, he'll be sitting with us, we always dine together."

Joel turned away, he pondered on what he'd just said. Before Bicknor he'd have said 'we always eat together,' yet without thinking he said 'dine'. He wondered if Constantine was changing him.

Constantine Ellis got out of the back of the blue Rover slowly and carefully. Joel took hold of his arm to help him.

"You OK? How did it go?"

"Uncomfortably, they wanted me to keep me there for a few days but I refused."

"Why?"

"I feel safer with you around me."

"Don't be stupid! By the way we drew on the Bounty Bars, two letters each."

"Help me up the stairs will you, walking's a bit painful at the moment."

"What about eating?"

"Can you ask the chef to send me something up, need some time to resume normal. What was her name in the end?"

"Calypso."

"As you guessed, there's some black blood in her somewhere."

"She says she'll buy the Bounty Bars."

"We'll hold her to that, give me a week to get on my feet again."

It took a while to slowly coax Connie up the curling stairs, get him into his room and comfortable in his bed. Connie wouldn't let Joel take his trousers off. Joel was worried she'd have finished and gone before he could get back.

"OK going down to order your food. Shepherds Pie or Liver and Onions?"

"What did she have?"

"Liver and Onions."

"I'll have the same then, What about sweet?"

"Ice cream of lemon sorbet."

Lemon sorbet sounds just the ticket."

"Drink?" Joel asked.

"No, I've got water here."

He put his hand on Connie's shoulder.

"Have you got pain killers?"

"Yes, Tramadol and Diclofenac but I'm not going to take them or I'll end up like you."

"How do you know about those drugs?"

"Is she dining with you?"

"Yes, so I'm going to go back down now and give your order to chef."

"OK, please pass on my apologies for not attending. I don't want to be a 'gooseberry'."

Joel looked defensively down a furrowed brow at his friend. It was though Constantine could instantly detect a threat to their friendship.

"Don't be silly, I'll check in on you before I go to bed."

"It's OK, I'll be fine." - There was a pause - "Really."

She was still there, just about to finish her sorbet.

"Sorry about that, he wasn't very mobile so had to help him upstairs and into bed."

"What's your friend's name?" Calypso asked.

"Constantine, Constantine Ellis."

"Sounds very Eton and Oxford."

"Cambridge actually,"

"And you?" Her perfect eyebrows raised as deep brown eyes questioned him.

"Private tutors, but not what you think."

"And do you know what I think Joel?" Once again their eyes settled for a long time.

"Maybe, a little bit." She laughed and the whole world laughed with her. Or that's how it seemed to Joel.

"Do you want to tell me?" She asked, putting down the coffee cup she'd just raised to her lips. "I can't drink this, I'll never sleep."

"Maybe tomorrow." He replied

"Living tomorrow where in the world will I be? Tomorrow." She sang quietly so only he could hear.

"Bee Gees, Now I've found that the world is round."

"I'm impressed." she laughed.

"Don't be, it's a very popular song at the moment, on the radio all the time."

"Don't spoil it, let me be impressed." Her smile and eyes demolished him. "Booze, I'm here for booze, unwanted little rich girl who drinks too much, so they farmed me out to here."

"Who are they?"

"Tell you tomorrow. I need to find my room now and try to sleep, usually have one or two or perhaps three nightcaps to help me do that but I suppose that's out of the question here."

"Just about everything's out of the question here."

"Not everything, surely?" Her eyes flashed in fun.

"Well you are allowed to go to the toilet on your own."

"What about our rooms, are there cameras?"

"No, but there are on the landings, stairs and communal areas."

"What if I want a fuck?"

Joel almost fell back as her bluntness hit him.

"Think you have to get written permission."

"You'd better buy a pen then, or better still borrow one." She laughed as she rose from the table.

Joel rose as she moved away from the table and towards the door. She turned and looked back.

"Show me 'round tomorrow?"

"Now I've found, that the world is round, and of course it rains everyday." Joel lyrically spoke the lines."

"In between the showers then."

She smiled then puckered her lips to a distant kiss before disappearing from Joel and the almost empty dining room.

Joel knocked and entered without waiting for any response or permission. In his left hand was a Earl Grey tea on a Royal Worcester cup and saucer. Constantine didn't take sugar so there was no spoon.

"Hey, posh boy, here's some tea, time to wake up." He moved to the curtains and drew them back, light flooded in from the green fields. Putting his arm around the recumbent Constantine Joel gently lifted his slight bony body up and positioned the pillows behind him.

"How are you feeling?"
"Bloody awful."
"You should have stayed in for a few days like they said."
"Yes but I had no friends there, they were all nice to me for money, it was their job."
"Here's the same."
"No it's not, you're here, you didn't bring my tea for money, for a wage."
"No, but I do get something out of our relationship."
"What?"

Joel paused for thought looking out of the large window at the hay bales with crows standing on them'

"I get to learn some Latin."
"Oh - 'In absentia lucis, Tenebrae vincunt' "
"And that means?"
"In the absence of light, darkness prevails."
"Exactly, now, drink your tea before it gets cold."
"How was dinner with Calypso?"
"OK, I'm going to show her around this morning."

Constantine glanced over towards Joel who was still deliberately looking out of the window.
"Are you going to show her our 'secret place'?"
"Maybe, see how it goes."
"Show her the pigs and chickens instead."
"That's a bit mean."

"Sorry, yes it is."

"Anyway I've found another secret place."

"Where?"

"Well it wouldn't be a secret if I told you, I'll show you when you're up to it."

Joel turned toward him and smiled. Constantine was so attractive in a languid way. Why wasn't he married?

"You're such a tease Joel, get out, go and fraternise with your exotic Calypso."

"You're feeling better then."

"A little, thanks for the tea."

He left the room, closed the door quietly and headed down for breakfast wondering if she would be there. Jonathan was 'hovering' between his office and the dining room waiting at the bottom of the stairs.

"A quick word if I may, Mr. Joel."

"In your office?"

"No here will do, I've had notification that a Mr. Edenson will be visiting this afternoon to see you. E,T.A, about two if you could be around."

"Oh! I'll have to cancel Cheltenham Races then that's a blow."

Jonathan looked disdainfully at him, his eyes peering through the slit between the top of his glasses and the deep furrows of his brow.

"If I'm correct Mr. Joel your visitor is the source of your funding here so it may be prudent to treat the visit more seriously."

Joel's usually amenable countenance stiffened.

"Mr. Edenson usually requires me to do very nasty things Mr. Jonathan, his benevolence comes at a very high price."

There was silence and a mutual glare.

"Two o'clock Mr. Joel, please be available." Jonathan turned and went into his office.

She was sitting at 'their' table in the same seat as last night.

"Good morning Miss Calypso, may I join you?"

"Please do Mr. Joel. I trust you slept well."

"No, my lover kept me awake."

"Oh! How romantic, what's his name?"
"Oxana."

There was engagement that lasted too long.

"Funny I slept very well, didn't expect to as there was no psychoactive drug to help me but for some reason I felt elated and went to sleep quickly."
"It's the air and the magnetic resonance of being encircled by moving water."
"Probably. What are you eating?"
"Devilled kidneys and poached egg on toast. I have the same every morning. Constantine says I'll get fat but no sign of it as yet."
"What else does Constantine say?"
"He says it's great that you're buying the Bounty Bars."
"You're lying."
"I am, It'll take him a few days to get back on his feet. Says he's looking forward to meeting you."

Calypso smiled.

"Miss Calypso - scrambled eggs!" Came the shout from the other side of the hatch.
"That'll be me then." She uncurled from the chair and moved towards the hatch. Her jeans supported her just enough to make his eyes and his mind wander.

"What are you going to show me first?"
"It's a secret, but you'll need to wear something sensible on your feet rather than elegant black stilettos."

She noted that he'd missed nothing.

"They're my 'fuck me now' shoes. Do you like them?"
"Very much." She laughed and cut into her toast.

There were seven people in the dining room, all suffering in some way or another. The winter morning glass clear sun streamed through the tall windows and fell across them, helping and brightening their morning struggle.

Coffee and immediate conversation had been finished.

"Come on then let's go, grab a warm coat and some trainers, it's not far."
"OK, I'm all yours, lead the way."

It was as though every comment was a suggestive innuendo, a comedy to disguise the tragedy of her life. That was why she was here. Thought Joel.

It was half past nine when she reappeared in the hall. A dark blue woolen short coat perfectly complemented her blue jeans that were tight in the right places, underneath a white silky polo neck shirt come jumper concealed her thirty five year old mellowing frame.

"How do you feel?" Joel asked.
"Shit." She answered without looking at him. "You?"
"Nervous, I've got some arsehole from MI5 coming to see me this afternoon. Constantine would eat him alive, they're on the same Eton, Oxbridge level but I'm just a country boy, a world apart. Come on this way."

They crossed the square diagonally to the left hand rear corner to the left of the little stone church and then turned left up the rough, slightly rising track. On their right was a derelict small stone building with sagging roof tiles and a half open door protected by impenetrable brambles.

"Do you think that was once someone's home?" She asked.
"Don't know, not sure, I would think more likely to be some kind of workshop or store, perhaps a blacksmiths or something."

To the left the ground rose steeply, almost a mound, covered in small trees and plants. An indistinct, little used earth pathway snaked through it.

"Come on, up here." He climbed up onto the bank, turned and offered his hand. She looked at him then took his hand. They both knew how enormous the moment was as their hands and eyes touched. She hadn't felt such care and emotion since Jonny in the painted ceiling room at Bovington. It was the same but different.

They climbed carefully for a few moments up the slippy, sometimes muddy-leafy half track til stone steps appeared a few yards before an black iron gate covered in the green veil of encroaching nature. Joel pushed it open against resistant hinges and gravity. A gravel path led away to the top of the mound. A secret graveyard of the Vaillancourt family, unkempt, overgrown, only manicured when it was time for another passing. In the centre was a tiny old stone chapel, it's heavy old oak door not locked and slightly open giving access to the dry inside. Ten pews and a small pulpit was the place where the family said their final farewells. Confident in their faith, comforted by their belief in eternal life.

Joel and Calypso stood silently in the dusty, leafy neglected chapel. Each drinking in the tangible history of the tiny place, shaping it as it permeated into their souls and bodies.

"Wow. It's beautiful, incredible, makes you wonder who has shed tears in here."

Joel moved up beside her and held the little finger of her left hand.

"What do you want to do?" Joel asked. They both stared at the simple wooden cross and figurine housed in a stone recess on the stone wall. Behind the cross was a discarded Mars bar wrapper.

"No idea but it makes our little struggles seem so selfish and silly."
"You're right of course but it doesn't make them any easier, we still feel like shit most of the time."
"It's easier with you around." she said, turning towards him. "Do you think it would offend them if we had a little kiss?"
"I don't think they're in any position to object. Close your eyes."

Joel looked at her olive face framed by her cosseting hair, the texture of the skin on her nose and mouth, the curl of her eyelashes. Slowly he closed in on her lips till they gently and silently touched. That was all that was needed, a few seconds of gentle sensual bliss altered both of their lives. It was almost as though they had come in as two and would leave as one. Without speaking they moved hand in hand outside, standing, looking, reading the individual headstones of the Vaillancout dynasty. Moving the avaricious vegetation to reveal dates and lives. Looking out from the mound to silent eternal peace.

"We'd better head back." Calypso said, staring at a headstone from 1818. "I've got a therapy session this afternoon."
"Do they help?"
"I suppose so, at least it's a diversion from your lone personal struggle."
"What about acupuncture?" Joel asked.
"Not sure, there's this mystical Chinese connection system which science has yet to prove exists. Maybe it's just a placebo thing, you know, a pain gain thing, I'm having sharp needles stuck into me so there must be a benefit. How about you."
"Like you I'm unsure but when I go to the toilet, you know, have a shit, I often get this twinge, no it's not a twinge it's like an electric pulse in the right side of my body, just for a second, but it's happened so many times and in the same place that it can't be a coincidence. As far as i know there's no connection between my bowels and the skin midway on my right side so who knows."
"Are you always so romantic?"
"Only when I'm in love."

She stopped in front of him on the descending earthy path and turned towards him.

"And are you in love?"

"Maybe, possibly, perhaps, beautiful women are usually high maintenance, expensive and trouble, so I'll have to think about it."

"You're in luck then. I'm not beautiful."

"Oh yes you are."

Joel lay on his bed staring at the ceiling, it was white, the walls were whiter than white, almost a glare, a sun that never set, He should get out of here and marry Sandra, she was safe, she'd take care of their money, even possibly save some. He'd never have any money with Calypso, not because she asked for it or even wanted it but he'd do and buy lavish things for her simply because of the path she walked in life. The path she walked through the world. No, he needed to marry Sandra quickly before he became a lost soul, or was he lost already, had he already lost?

Trevor the nurse knocked at his door.

"Visitor downstairs for you Mr. Joel. In Mr. jonathan's office."

"OK Trevor, thank you, five minutes."

Joel got up from his bed, put on his shoes and splashed some water over his face. Edensone could wait a few minutes, he'd check in on Constantine first.

He knocked gently in case he was asleep then peeped around the door.

"Hello you, how are you feeling today?"

"Where have you been? I've been lonely all morning."

"Showing Calypso secret place two."

"Have you shown her secret place one yet?"

"No, I'm saving that for you."

"I'm not besotted by her."

"Neither am I."

Constantine cast a 'look' at Joel.

"Got to go, do you think you'll make dinner tonight?"

"Yes, I need to rescue my special friend from Ms. Calypso. Why have you got to go?"

"Horrible Edenson's here, my controller from MI5, wish you were able to come with me, he's on your level."

"What do you mean, 'my level'?"

"You know, Eton / Oxbridge level."

"Oh! Find out what his thesis was in?"

"Why? Is that important."

"Yes, it'll tell us a lot. Off you go, and remember, he needs you, just as much as you need him."

Joel reached onto the bed and squoze Connie's hand before leaving.

It was an immaculate dark blue suit, cream shirt and tasteful purple tie. It was a uniform. He'd recently had a haircut. His round affable face hid his true feelings and intentions. He sat relaxed with legs crossed in the leather armchair opposite Mr. Jonathan's desk. He'd taken over the office. Mr. Jonathan was now a lackey that supplied coffee, tea and polite time filling conversation.

"Well you look a lot better than the last time we met."

"That's because I'd just come back from the dead the last time we met."

Edenson glanced at Jonathan as much as to say - 'see what I've got to deal with'.

"I'll leave you to chat." Jonathan pushed back from his desk and left the room.

"How are you feeling?"

"Shit most of the time with the occasional good day."

"Mr. Jonathan tells me you're down to ten mill a day now, that's good. Another month should see you right."

"Right for what?"

"Right for this." Edenson reached down into a large brown leather briefcase and pulled out a thick manila file bound with thick rubber bands, three of them. Both the front and back of the file were stamped 'Secret'.

"What's that?"

"Information on two of our top fast jet pilots, the best of the best. They're both now dead unfortunately. The one, Jolyon Clay, almost certainly was trying to defect to the U.S.S.R. with one of our Lightning interceptors equipped with the very latest radar. He was stopped, shot down by another Lightning over Russian Airspace. The pilot of that Lightning was a Mr. Jonny Conrad who happened to be the best friend of Clay, so much so that he was Mr. Clay's best man at his wedding. Jonny Conrad subsequently committed suicide, we presume because of his required action in protecting the security of our nation."

"So what's that got to do with me?"

"Nothing as yet, it's background information you need to know. Both pilots were friends with a woman called Henrietta Betts. Betts is a founder member and a chief strategist and very active activist of CND. It is thought that she persuaded Clay to defect and we're worried that she is targeting key military personnel in order to bring about a socialist single state communist government to this country. Her publicly stated aim is to bring about the end of Capitalism and thus war."

"So what do you want me to do? Kill her."

"Yes, but that won't be easy, she's heavily protected by CND personnel wherever she goes, they're fully aware that 'accidents' may happen. So we need someone like you, someone who's been to prison, someone from the other side of the tracks as it were, to help us."

"What's in it for me?"

"The usual, an increase in pension and we'll buy you a reasonable house in the country somewhere. Your choice."

"So I'm now just an expendable hitman?"

"If you wish to be basic, yes."

"And afterwards, what if you want to 'expend' me?"

"People like you Mr. Joel are always, - shall we say - useful. Study the file, be careful with it, it is a 'secret' document. I'll drop by again in about a month to check on your welfare."

Edenson's eyebrows raised at his own insincerity.

"What's the current 'preferred method'?" Joel asked.

"Well we're currently trialling an umbrella that fires a micro engineered pellet full of Ricin, it seems quite effective on pigs."

"Is Henrietta Betts a pig?"

"Mr. Joel, she has been instrumental in the deaths of two highly trained expensive pilots and is agitating for the removal of our country's nuclear deterrent. Somehow I don't see Russia throwing all it's nuclear bombs into the Moskva river, do you?"

"No, they've shipped them all to Cuba, Oh! Sorry they've shipped them all back again after we nearly caused nuclear armageddon. Perhaps she's right?"

"See you in a month Mr. Joel. You take good care of yourself." It wasn't a platitude, it was a threat.

Edenson rose from the chair and left. Joel could hear him muttering to Jonathan in the hall.

He sat in the chair wondering whether to speak to Constantine, Calypso or no one. He needed his medicine today. He quickly made for the door.

"Mr. Edenson." Edenson turned as he reached the door.

"Oxford or Cambridge?"

"Oxford."

"What did you take?"

"Economics."

"What was your thesis on?" Edenson looked perplexed and irritated.

"The economic relevance of research budgets in the long term development of the armament industry." He snapped, "why?" He failed to see the point in Joel's question and was losing patience.

"Just wondered." Edenson turned and left.

Chapter 8.

Secret - for MI5 Eyes only:-

Surveillance Aldermaston March Sunday 29th March 1964 (5 mile radius)

There were two and a half pages of car numbers, the highlighted one read,

SCJ 448 - *pale metallic green Sunbeam-Talbot Alpine drophead tourer. - Jolyon Vernon Clay, Bovington Hall Herefordshire - note Clay is a current serving RAF Pilot Officer undergoing pilot training at RAF Cranwell. See attached report.*

Joel flipped over to the report at the back of the file. ------*although the owner of this vehicle could not be verified on the day, a surveillance target - Miss Henrietta Betts (believed to be the secretary and prime organiser of activities of CND - known as Hetty Betts) made her way back to this vehicle. The young male driver was waiting for her but had not taken part in the march /rally. A covert follow of her in this vehicle led to number 47 Henry Street Walsall, the parental home of Pilot Officer Jonny Conrad. Clay and Conrad are on the same flying course and are billeted together at Cranwell.*

Joel fell asleep, the file fell onto the floor.

The knocking on his door didn't wake him up but the shaking of his shoulder did, a seemingly thinner, white faced Constantine stood before him.

"Dinner time, what's this?" Connie picked up the splayed file and shuffled it back into its folder.

" - Secret - MI5 Eyes only - Is there something you haven't told me my beautiful boy?"
"There's lots I haven't told you Connie and lot's you wouldn't want to know."
"Try me someday, I might surprise you." The two young men looked at each other, one fully aware of the innuendo, one not sure.

"Come on, Trevor will be here in a minute for your swab, spruce yourself up and let's go down to dinner Lamb chops, mint sauce, fake new potatoes from Israel what more could a chap ask for."

"You're obviously feeling a lot better then?"

"Yes and can't wait to meet your Miss Calypso."

"She's not 'MY' Miss Calypso."

"Are you sure about that? I think she's got you dangling, how does the song go? *She's got you dangling on a string, break it and she won't care.*"

"Dancing!"

"What?"

"It's *dancing on a string,* not dangling."

Connie smiled.

"Won't you take this advice I hand you like a brother?
Or are you not seeing things too clear?
Are you too much in love to hear?
Is it all going in one ear and out of the other."

Joel lunged at him as he rolled off the bed but Connie was way too quick for him, his thin body arching away, his handsome gaunt face laughing. It was the first time Joel had heard him laugh.

"Better forget her." Connie touched his arm and looked directly into his eyes.

Joel looked away, he didn't want to but felt he ought to.

"How about you Connie? Anyone special you're trying to forget?"

"Nobody - until now that is - plenty of stuff in my past I really want to forget but never will, until I sought it."

"What do you mean?"

"Come on, I'm hungry, let's have a bet on what colour she'll be wearing?"

"OK, I'm going for - a dark green." Joel stated.

"Umm, by now she's getting confident in her surroundings and wants to show off, I'm going for yellow."

"No yellow won't suit her skin, you've lost already."

Connie slapped him gently on the shoulder.

"Let's see shall we, 'secret agent'."

She was sitting at 'their' table. Joel thought she'd lost weight in just the few days she'd been here. Maybe it was the lack of alcohol tightening up the looseness of her skin, maybe it was the long walks they'd been on, trying to glimpse the small herds of deer that tripped silently through the surrounding woods. Whatever, she looked absolutely beautiful in a fawn tight skirt and pale lemon satin blouse. The colours really suited her. Her hair was always perfect, however she positioned it around her face. Her eye makeup almost invisible but absolutely complementary to her deep deep eyes.

"Calypso, this is Mr. Constantine Ellis."

Calypso remained seated, smiled and accepted Constantine's hand before the two men sat down. There was an immediate leveling of understanding. There was no need for the niceties of smalltalk.

"Joel tells me you're here to rid yourself of the need for fine Irish Whisky."

Calypso looked at Joel.

"Does he tell you everything Mr Ellis?"
"No, he tells me very little, please call me 'Connie' Miss Calypso."
"Is he your lover?" She asked.

It was as though Joel wasn't at the table. Connie looked into her eyes.

"No, -- not yet."
"So, what about you Constantine Ellis? Why are you at this beautiful place?" She asked.

"Calypso - pork pie salad!" Yelled the voice from the kitchen.

"I'll get it for you Calypso." Joel said, rising from his chair. She smiled her thanks.

"I was a diplomat in Istanbul, I got injured in an incident so I'm here having the odd bit of surgery at Birmingham and generally recuperating."
"Really?" Her body, face and words questioned him. "I think it's a lot more serious than that.!" She stared at him over a cut glass beaker of water as Joel positioned her salad plate in front of her.
"Thank you darling." She touched his hand and looked happily into his face before moving her attention back to Connie.

"Is that your green Bristol parked around the back?"
"Yes, why?"
"Thought so, I'm a Lotus girl myself."
"They're OK for a short swift jolly but not suitable for the long haul. - are they Joel?"

Connie deliberately brought Joel back into the conversation.

"I'm not an expert on cars, mother had an old Citroen deux chevaux. A van called an Arcadian." Joel noticed himself changing his words, normally he'd have said - Mum had a - but here, in these surroundings with these people 'mum' sounded wrong.

Connie laughed."An umbrella on four wheels."

Calypso immediately rallied to Joel's side.

"Can you drive darling?" Claiming possession of his right hand with her left, making sure Connie could see.

"Don't know, never tried."

"I'll teach whilst we're here. Constantine may we borrow your Bristol?" She asked.
"No, certainly not, it's far too sophisticated for a learner."

She immediately countered his rebuff.

"I'll buy you something, a Mini or something cheap to learn in."

"Lamb Chops, Mr Joel Mr. Ellis." The voice rang out.

"Do you always have the same?" Calypso asked Connie.
"Always, we're joined at the hip, hadn't you noticed." He laughed, rose from the table before Joel had time to move and placed his hand on Joel's shoulder as he passed. "You stay there, I'll get our dinner."

The food, as always, was delicious. The conversation, rapacious and full of innuendo with knowing smiles, occasional laughter accompanied by possessive touching. The water could have been champagne, the orange juice brandy. They were the last people in the dining room. Joel knew he'd have to choose which room to sleep in and that choice could affect the rest of his life. He decided it was safer to choose his own. To sleep with the King and not a queen.

The 'Secret' file lay on his bedside table, like schoolboy homework waiting to be done. Each night he'd glance at it then shove it away, out of reach but never out of mind.

' Betts is the founder and principal leader of 'The Island' a registered charity whose mission statement is to provide temporary respite, advice and counselling for female victims of domestic violence. It maintains a substantial property in the district of Sale in Manchester. Records indicate that Clay purchased and financially supported the upkeep, running costs and maintenance of this property. It is believed that the house could become a serious source of information for Betts as 'wronged' wives reveal facts about their respective husbands.

'Surely that was a good thing to do.' Joel thought to himself as his eyes closed.

"Come on young man, it's stopped raining, come and show me this 'other' secret place of yours. I don't want 'her' to be ahead of me."
"It's not a contest Connie."
"Oh yes it is. Come on, shoes and coat."
"It's not far, it's sort of hiding in plain sight. Just behind the workshops."

Joel and Constantine crossed the big square, left up the track, up the steep slippy mound to the steps and the black metal gate.

"You'd just walk by this, without knowing it existed." Connie looked taken back by the miniature hidden cemetery with its stone, small, very private chapel made so, so, special by the dead leaves that had blown in through the open door and the undisturbed dust. The most recent grave was an old woman, the name suggested she'd been matriarch of the family. Died at the age of ninety two.

"Emily Astor Vaillancourt, 1860 - 1952. Wonder what she was like?"
"Privileged." Joel quietly said. "Probably never did a hard day's work in her life."
"You don't know that Joel, She may have been a nurse in the Crimean war."
"Too young, it finished in 1856. And too old for the first world war."
"Since when have you been a historian Joel?"
"Since a green dilapidated gypsie van in Wales with a very knowledgeable man who taught me everything he knew ----- which was a lot."
"What was his name?"
"Edvin loach."
"Is he still alive?"
"I don't know, he brought a horse, a Welsh Cob and moved on."

The grave stones got older til they were so old you couldn't read the dates, just bits of names. Joel and Constantine stood in silence just looking and thinking. Connie took hold of Joel's hand. It was a dark place surrounded by light.

"Has she brought you a car?"

"Yes."

"What sort?"

"A Mini like she said."

"What colour?"

"Green."

"Have you fucked her yet?"

"No."

"Are you going to?"

"I expect so, it's expected and to be honest I get a hard on every time we're together."

"What about me? Do you get a hard on with me?"

"Only when you touch me."

"Can I touch you in the Chapel?"

"No. It doesn't seem right."

"They castrated me you know. They were all drunk, twelve of them, they had a contest, who had the biggest cock, the smallest went first, they tied me down over a big table, my wrists and legs to the legs of the table, then all of them did it, laughing, measuring their cocks with a ruler to decide the order of entry as you might say. The only one who didn't do it was their captain, Captain Sosa was his name. He had a huge dog, a Kuchi guard dog from Afghanistan, it never left his side. After the soldier with the biggest cock had raped me he took out a cut throat razor, sliced into my scrotum and cut out my balls, I was passing in and out of consciousness with the pain. I was unconscious so they threw a bucket of cold piss over my head. Sosa yanked my head up by my hair and made me watch as he threw my bloody balls to the dog, who ate them in one gulp."

Constantine Ellis Collapsed onto one of the small dusty pews sobbing tears that were full of relief.

"I've never told that to anyone Joel, not even the therapists here. No one, how could one, unless the person was very special to you. Put your arms around me Joel and kiss me. Make me feel worthwhile."

Joel sat down next to his sobbing friend and put his arms around the thin convulsive man that huddled up to him. It was a kiss of compassion on Connie's cheek. Despite his sobbing Connie noticed the bulge in Joel's trousers and stroked it. After a while there was a wet patch.

"Who were they?" Connie.

Turkish soldiers, well not really soldiers members of MIT."

"What's MIT?"

"Milli Istihbarat Teskilati, the secret service, the Turkish equivalent of the Russian KGB. I was lecturing at the Institute for Research on Turkish Culture, locally it was known as the TKAE in downtown Ankara, it was my cover, employed by the British Council as an expert on Claudius Ptolemy and his scientific influence on the Byzantine empire."

"And are you?"

"Am I what?"

"An expert on that?"

"Yes of course, I told you before I was fairly 'fringe' at Cambridge. Anyway, the aim was to disrupt the 'entente cordiale' between Russia and Turkey. The Americans were very active in Turkey fielding a lot of people under the guise of anti-narcotics advisors and trainers, really they were simply spreading American influence, propaganda and spying, they didn't give a toss about the trade in narcotics, in fact the CIA were actively profiting from it, just like they're doing in Vietnam. I'd formed a friendship with a young Nationalist activist called Enver."

"Just a friendship?" Joel's question was humorous but pertinent.

"Just a friendship, remember I had balls then. Enver worked as a journalist for the Ankara edition of the daily *Yeni Istanbul*, It was an open secret that the TKAE served as a rallying point firstly against left wing activism in Turkey and secondly, which was more important for me, against Russia. Anyway, through Enver I was introduced to a Russian called Volkod, he was an official at the Russian Embassy in Istanbul. Volkod was a passport officer but his real job was assistant director of the Russian Intelligence network in Turkey, so he had a lot of information and was a very big fish. London was very keen to get him out. Istanbul was and still is a hotbed of espionage, you can't trust anybody, nobody is who they seem to be. Volkod and his petrified wife had tasted life in the West at the Paris Embassy, he wanted out but she was so scared, she knew that even if they made it out safely all their families back in Russia would be rounded up and shot, simply as a warning to anyone else. It was no light undertaking. I became the 'go between' between Volkod and a chap called Michael Elliot who was the head of MI6 in the Istanbul Embassy. The current Ambassador at the time wanted nothing to do with spying or espionage at the time and barely tolerated Elliot, he considered it dirty and underhand, not the sort of thing British Officers should be doing."

Constantine leaned forward onto his folded arms resting on the back of the little pew.

"The date was to be April the 3rd, It was towards the end of the 'Philby' era, his misguided socialistic leanings had killed a lot of people and very nearly killed me. The plan was that Volkod and his wife should wait outside the entrance to the Basilica Cistern as if they were tourists If all was well and they were ready to go they should carry a Bim supermarket bag. Anyway they were there with their bag. I instructed the taxi driver to close in on them and stop for them to get in. He did this but as soon as he pulled up three black Ford Consuls immediately boxed us in. All of us were arrested by armed MIT men including the taxi driver, he'd gone white and was on his knees begging that he was an innocent taxi driver and knew nothing.

They believed him and let him go. Volkod was by now standing like a statue trembling, his wife was in hysterics on the floor, the men literally threw her into the back of one of the cars, handcuffed myself and Volkod to an officer and pushed us into separate cars. Off we went to what turned out to be a secret MIT office near Genclik Park. All three cars drove straight into a heavily guarded basement and then it started. They knew exactly what was happening from the information Philby had passed to his Russian handler in london. Philby was best friends with Elliot both Eton and Cambridge, so he knew everything. The Russians had passed it onto the Turkish Authorities simply as a gesture to promote cooperation and of course to get the Turkish MIT to do their dirty work for them. They dragged Volkod and his wife out of the cars and shot them in the head there and then. They knew they were trying to defect and so hadn't had a chance to pass over any information so there was no point in torturing them for information. They had their contact. Me, I was pretty scared, I assumed I would be tortured then killed. They locked me up in an underground cell for two days whilst they waited to see what the political fall out would be from my disappearance, in other words how important was I? Apparently it was considerable, it had been leaked to the papers and questions were being asked. They handed me over to their goons and you know the rest."

"How on earth did you escape?"

"Don't think I was supposed to, either that or they didn't care either way, they just left me tied to that table bleeding and passing in and out of consciousness. Early the next morning a woman cleaner came into the room, she didn't seem at all surprised to find me there, I got the feeling she'd seen it all before, a few times. She did seem surprised that I was still alive. She untied my hands and nodded towards a door, then left, I was so weak it was a real struggle to undo the rope around my ankles. There was a lot of blood on the floor, my blood. The door was one of those emergency exits with a bar, I pushed it and it opened, it led up some steps, into a rear garden then out through a gate. I must have collapsed in the street, half naked, just a shirt, covered in blood. The next thing I knew I was in hospital."

"So what now?"

"Lunch, I'm cold and hungry but thank you for listening."

Constantine kissed Joel on his cheek as he stood up.

"No I mean what now? What do you want to do."

"It's not a case of what I want to do Joel, It's a case of what I'm going to do. I'm going to kill Captain Sosa and his fucking dog."

Joel sensed and saw an element of absolute steel in the man he was beginning to love.

Chapter 9.

It arrived on the back of a flatbed Ford Transit, shiny Almond Green with a white roof, the motif on the back read *'Austin Seven'*. The wheels looked so small.

"It's a new lawnmower for the house." Connie joked as the man operated the winch and the Mini rolled obediently down. Calypso took the keys from the man and handed them to Joel with a smile and a kiss. Jonathan viewed the scene from the window of his office, some other residents came out of the front door to look. C970 DJW was the number.

"It smells like a new car." Joel said grinning.
"It is a new car, have a sit in."

Joel sat on the driver's seat, it was grey and green. He looked around, tried the little chrome door handle come lever that hid inside the empty door space, a huge compartment ran the whole length of the lower door. The controls seemed simple, dominated by a round black and white speedo in the middle of an oval binnacle. A long wand of a gear stick came out of the floor. He put the key in the simple lock directly under the binnacle and turned it, lights came on but nothing else happened. The garage driver leaned on the open drivers door and looked in.

"You have to press that big button on the floor but don't do it yet, put the handbrake on."
"Where's that?" enquired an excited Joel.
"It's that black lever between the seats, just pull it up to put the handbrake on then press the white button in to put it down and release the brake."

Joel pulled it up and listened to the clicking of the ratchet.

"Now check it's in neutral."
"What do you mean?" The man raised his eyebrows towards Calypso.
"It's got four forward gears and one reverse gear, we have to make sure it's not in any gear before we start the engine, think of it like a letter 'H' and the cross bit is 'neutral' look there's a little diagram on the top of the gear stick.

Calypso intervened.

"It's OK I'll teach him later, do you need me to sign anything?"

The man withdrew from the Mini to the cab of his Transit and emerged with a clipboard.

"Just a signature here Ma'am if you don't mind and I'll be on my way. Lovely place you've got here."

"Yes it is, isn't it?" Calypso went along with his misunderstanding. The man and his truck left.

Connie got into the little green car.

"Come on, let me show you how to drive." Said Connie.

Joel glanced at Calypso for unspoken permission. There was a barely perceptible nod and smile. He got in the passenger's side.

"Right, pay attention, the left hand pedal is the clutch you need to press that down before you put it in any gear. The middle pedal is the brake and the pedal on the right is the accelerator. Use your right foot for the accelerator and brake and your left foot for the clutch. All the clutch does is disengage or engage the engine and gearbox. Now, cheap cars like this don't have what's called a 'synchromesh' on the first gear, so if I just press the clutch and put it into first gear it will make a horrible crunching noise which is not good for your gearbox so the trick is to press the clutch twice or better still put it into second gear then slide it back into first. Watch!"

"I can drive a tractor."

Connie glanced a disparaging look.

"Hardly the same is it?"

Calypso was watching as the two young men sat in the car she'd just bought for him. The little engine jumped noisily into life before it moved off up the long drive shuddering and skitting like a marble rolling over a rough road. She felt like the mother of two young rascals and hoped it would come back safely. When it returned it's progress was jerky and hesitant but the young driver's smile lit up her world.

"You'll have to get a licence, then have a few lessons then take a test." Calypso said as they both stood looking at the green car now parked safely around the back. Constantine had gone in for a sleep.

"No I won't, I'll just make a phone call, you can teach me here till my licence turns up then we'll ask Mr. Jonathan if we can go out on a few trips."

Calypso gave him a 'confused' look.

"My services don't come cheap, but seeing as it's you I'll accept payment in kind, ---------- I'd like the first payment now please."

Joel could see her breathing becoming more urgent.

"Right now?"
"Right now."

Joel felt the keys and something else hard in his pocket. He wasn't sure which excited him the most.

He'd never been in her room before. It was white like his but her curtains were floral, somehow it was a woman's room.

She sat on the soft pale pink bed.

"Undress me slowly and carefully, fold my clothes up and put them on that chair."

Joel stood in front of her and complied, holding him she rubbed his wetness all over her breasts and nipples before pulling him down to his knees to lick and suck.

"I want it in now, I can't wait any longer."

Somehow the winter afternoon sun had a glare that cut across the room and drew moving lines on the wall. Calypso and Joel lay naked side by side relaxed and fulfilled.

"Nearly as good as Irish whisky." She chuckled to him.
"It's the wrong colour and apparently there's only ten CC's of it."
"Any chance of a fill up? I'm thirsty." She turned her head to immerse her whole self into his eyes.

Joel rolled onto his knees, sitting over her breasts, watching as she made him grow ever closer to her lips.

The sun had gone now, darkness was galloping towards them, their happiness made Joel hum a tune as they lay in each other's arms.

"In my White room with black curtains near the station." He sang.
"It's 'The' she whispered in his ear.

"What?"

"It's 'The' - In THE white room with black curtains near the station.' - "

"Are you sure?"

"Yes, I'm always right."

`   "In the white room with black curtains near the station,
        Black roof country, no gold pavements, tired starlings."

"There's some controversy over the last bit, some people hear it as 'tiny' starlings. What do you think?" Joel commented.

"Tired sounds more interesting."

"Yes I agree with you."

"How come you know this?"

"They came to stay for a week and played a lot of songs."

"Came where?"

"Luggala in Southern Ireland, where I live, it's a big country mansion, lots of famous groups and people come to stay for a rest, get away from it all sort of thing."

"Is that where you came from when you arrived in a helicopter?"

"Yes."

"Is Ginger Baker still on gear?"

"Very much so. I'm very wet, can you run me a nice hot bath and take me in the bathroom? Can you manage that?" She looked at him.

"This Mini's very expensive."

"All beautiful women are high maintenance and expensive, you should know that." She laughed as he left her bed and moved towards her bathroom.

'He should marry Sandra as soon as possible' he thought to himself as he got bigger again.

"I need a driving licence."

Mr. Jonathan pretended to be immersed in papers at his desk but was really listening to every word.

"Well apply for one like everybody else." Edenson curtly said.

"I can't can I.? I don't have a birth certificate thanks to you lot"

There was a silence and after a few seconds some muted conversation as though he was talking with his hand over the phone.

"About two weeks but it won't include HGV's or goods vehicles over 7.5 tons. In fact I'll probably bring it with me when I visit in three weeks time. What are you down to now?"

"Six mil."

"Ok, tell Mr. Jonathan I'll be visiting on December the third. Have you read that file yet?"
"Some of it."
"Yes well she's your next job, so make sure you know everything there is to know."

There was no goodbye or niceties, Edenson just put the phone down.

"Did you get that Mr. jonathan?"
"Yes, December the third, presumably in the afternoon, I'll put it in the diary."

There was no pretence as to privacy. The phone belonged to Bicknor Court as did everything said on it. 'Better read the rest of the file before Edenson turns up'. Joel thought to himself as he left the office.

Most mornings he'd spend with Connie. After breakfast they'd walk somewhere. Today they were going down to the river, along the bank for half a mile then into the little stone church, apparently it was only used for high days and holidays but it was always open and provided a secluded quiet place for the two young men who never ran out of conversation. It was a beautiful special place. Their place.

"Do you love her?" Connie asked, stretching out his legs to the side of the pew. The floor was old small black and white tiles made uneven by recurring floods that seasonally encroached.

"Depends what love is, if it's physical enjoyment of her soft delightful curves and deep fulfillment of my desires, I suppose I do. If it's total compatibility and peace, you know, someone you can just be with and not have to pretend anything, then no I don't, that would be Sandra."
"Sandra sounds nice."
"She's a fat vet with ginger frizzy hair. Or she will be when she's finished her course."
"Sandra sounds nice! I feel like that with you Joel, I don't have to pretend anything, you know most things about me."

"I'm not in your league Connie, I don't know Latin or anything about Greek Gods."

"That's why I love you." Connie turned towards Joel and slowly kissed him on the lips. Joel accepted his kiss, it didn't seem wrong.

After minutes of silence and thought Joel put his hand on Connie's.

"Come on, don't want to be late for lunch, cream of tomato soup and grilled pork."

"You know it's Thelma from the walled garden don't you?"

"No I didn't."

"They killed her two days ago, Louise is distraught without her. They'll kill Louise next month then start again with two small piglets."

"Maybe we shouldn't give them names."

"How about Sandra and Calypso?" Connie laughed.

"So, which one would you kill first Connie?"

"Calypso." Joel looked at Connie.

"Thought so. That's what I do you know?"

"What?"

"Kill people, Edenson tells me who and gives me the means to do it then I have to do it."

"What on earth are you talking about? Nobody has to kill anyone."

"I do Connie, if I don't do as they say they'll kill me because of what I know, you see I'm not recorded anywhere, there are no records of me. They could knock me off and get away with it, nobody would ask anything."

The two young men walked together in silence, up the steep rough track, past the Youth Hostel then up to the gates of Bicknor Court. Some of the winter leaves were still clinging on to brown bare sticks that barely moved in the breeze. Their siblings piled up and rustling on the ground, waiting for the wind to blow them into hidden heaps, the rain to decompose them back into nature's food. They stopped at the gates.

"Will you help me kill Sosa and his dog?"

There was a silence, and it was silent, no wind, no rain, no cars, no sound other than their breathing as they recovered from the steep climb.

"Of course. I'll do anything you ask me to."

They held hands as they walked but separated as they got close to the house.

If Calypso wasn't doing a therapy or working in the garden she liked Joel to spend the afternoons in her room. It had only taken him a week to master the Mini, going up and down the long private road to the cattle grid and back, reversing, three point turns then parking in the backyard. He found it all too easy, not too different from the tractor on the farm. Calypso always dressed nicely to accompany him in the Mini, even though they were going nowhere, by the time they'd been up and down the road a few times she'd let her hand stray and stroke the inside of his legs. Nothing was ever said as they went up to her room, sometimes she'd wear underwear, sometimes not. She liked to watch him naked doing things for her. It was a game they both enjoyed until she couldn't wait any longer. Afterwards there was Sandra and now Connie in his head. 'Where was his life going? He'd read the file properly tonight'.

"It's times like this I could really do with a drink." Calypso lay back naked on her soft bed.

"Times like what?"

"Times like after you've just fucked me. I'm like you, I can sense you mulling things over in your mind, people, relationships, your life in general, where is it heading? I'm the same, all this stuff floats to the surface."

"Have you always drunk a lot Calypso?"

"No, I was just a normal champagne drinking girl, hardly ever touched anything else."

"What changed?"

"My husband Jolyon got killed, crashed his jet fighter. I don't believe it for an instant, then my lover, someone a bit like you - killed himself, I'm sure it was something to do with Jolyon's death, they were best chums, been through training together. Jonny was Jolyon's best man at our wedding. Jolyon didn't mind sharing me with Jonny, he knew of course but we didn't speak about it. Jolyon was actually the father of my son Salvador, not Jonny. Jolyon came from a very rich old money family but he had some strange socialistic tendencies, almost as though he felt terribly guilty about being rich and privileged. Anyway through Jonny he met up with a horrible communist pygmy with curly short hair called Hetty Betts. He immediately hit it off with her, he became her taxi to CND marches and rallies, gave her money for various projects and generally became her best friend even though he was a serving pilot officer at the time. Everybody tried to talk him round but he was having none of it. He'd found his 'cause celebre' and that was socialism. The fact that it didn't work was lost on him. After our honeymoon in St. Petersburg he started communicating with Guy Burgess in Russia, apparently he was a dreadful drunk of a man. I met him once he looked dirty and smelt of garlic and booze. I'd kill Hetty Betts in an instant if I could, she's wrecked my life and has no idea. Apparently she turned up at Bovington Hall - my parents-in-law's house, wanting to know why Jolyon's money had stopped being paid to her project. She had no idea she'd almost without doubt killed him. Fuck me again Joel. Please! Make it all go away!."

Joel did as she wanted. His brain was whirling. Surely it couldn't be.

"Does Hetty Betts know you hate her and want to kill her?"
"Course not, she thinks we're all chums, what's left of us that is, i suppose it's just me really."

There it was, in black and white - Jolyon Vernon Clay, Bovington Hall Herefordshire. It was the same person. It took him til eleven at night to go through the file, mainly it was just logs of sightings and contacts. She was right Jolyon and Jonny seemed to share everything, including her.

Chapter 10.

It wasn't Edenson that got out of the car, it was an older man in his forties, thicker set with just the start of a gut. A pleasant face but there was something wrong, the smiling soft face somehow didn't match the aura.

"Good afternoon old chap I'm Mr. Holman, Peter Holman." Holman put out his hand as he approached the front door and Joel.

Joel shook it but it was a very brief contact as Holman quickly withdrew.

"Where's Edenson?"
"Not very well I'm afraid, in bed with flu. So here I am, beautiful place, never been here before, apparently in the war a Wellington bomber crashed in the valley below doing some experimental radar stuff, all killed I'm afraid, very fragile life isn't it?"
"Yes." Joel replied. Holman had obviously done his homework.

Joel led the way inside. Knocking as he entered he didn't bother introducing Holman to Mr. jonathan. They nodded to each other as Jonathan headed for the kitchen and then the walled garden to the pigs. Sandra and Calypso were getting quite big now. Joel suspected Mr. Jonathan preferred the company of the pigs to humans, that is before he had them killed.

Joel and Peter Holman sat in the two wooden chairs by the window.

"How are you feeling old chap?" It was the second time in minutes he's used the words, they began to grate. Joel was nothing but work to Holman, they both knew it.

"Strong."
"Ah! That's good then." It wasn't the reply he was expecting from a recovering addict.
"Have you read the file?"
"Yes."
"Then I'll take it back with me if you've finished with it."

"I said I'd read it, not finished with it, I'd like some more time with it if mind, just to get the detail."

"Ummm! I suppose that will be OK but normally we don't like 'Class out of the office for too long, if you know what I mean, so make sure you Ic Now the target-----"

"Hetty Betts." Joel interceded. Holman immediately stiffened.

"How on earth do you know she's known as 'Hetty'? It's not in the file.

"Like you Mr. Holman, I've been doing some homework, apparently the file I've got is only half the story." Joel blagged.

"It's all you need to know Mr. Joel. You'll find it difficult to get close to her. She's well 'guarded' shall we say by CND supporters, staff, security, call them what you will. That's why we need someone with rather an 'alternative' background."

"Is that it?"

Holman nodded towards a furled black Yve St. Laurent umbrella which he'd brought in with him.

"It fires a micro pellet containing Ricin poison, uses compressed air, so You only get one shot."

Holman reached over for the umbrella.

"Watch very carefully Mr. Joel."

In the handle was a dark green round dot, he slid it to the side, turned the handle ninety degrees and a small spring loaded plunger popped out.

"Press that and it's gone."
"What's the range?"
"Within one foot if possible."
"Will the target feel anything?"
"Maybe a little itch, rather like an insect bite, no pain."
Will it go through cloth?"
"Of course."
"Does it make a noise?"
"That I don't know, I've never fired one."
"How long will it take to work?"
"The target will be dead within thirty six hours."

Holman turned the handle to the right and pressed in the plunger, the green shutter slid back over it.

72

Joel stood up and stared out of the window. The land dropped gently away ,m the house towards the river. Everything was winter brown and the mat drab green of a grey day.

"I can get close to your target, with someone's help, it will take a while and I'll need three air tickets, in about a month when I've finished here."

"Where to?"

"Istanbul. And I'll need some diplomatic help when we're there."

"Who's we?"

"That's my business, but if you want me to get close to Betts it's necessary.-------for me."

"Be careful Mr. Joel, we don't allow the tail to wag the donkey for too long, if you get my drift. Time to go, hate night time car journeys."

"I'll see you out. Oh have you got anything for me?."

"Like what?"

"Like a Driving licence."

Holman screwed up his face, he'd forgotten, clicked open his briefcase, it was a reluctant , almost throwing down, of the little red book onto the desk.

"Thank you, the number of my Mini is C970 DJW, could you organise some insurance for me?"

There was an unpleasant silence as the two men stared at each other, Holman assessing if it was a battle he needed to fight. Joel assessing his unadmitted value to them.

"I'll have the number put on a Home Office list, you won't need insurance."

"Thank you Mr. Holman,-------------Peter."

Peter Holman wasn't impressed by the 'smart arse' druggie hippy standing before him. He strode deliberately quickly towards the door.

Joel walked the few yards behind the 'sprinting' Holman, out of the front door to the waiting car. It was a Daimler Jaguar saloon. Joel guessed that Holman was Edenson's boss. The unnoticeable driver opened the rear door, Holman got into the back.

"Look after that umbrella Mr. Joel, be very careful where you leave it."

"Business class tickets please Mr. Holman." Peter Holman wound up the window and the car quietly left.

"You've had a visitor." Constantine stroked Joel's shoulder as he sat on his bed.

"Yes.-------- Connie?"

"What."

"I want to help you."

"What do you mean? Help me with what?"

"I can help you kill Captain Sosa and his dog."

Constantine Ellis lay back on his bed and sighed.

"How on earth can you do that?"

"It's what I do, I've told you. My visitor came about a job for them. I said I had to do something for me first. By 'me' I mean you. You're not going to get better til this is sorted and I'd really like it if you were well."

"My darling beautiful Joel, my problems aren't your problems."

Connie pulled Joel backwards onto the bed, put his left arm under his head then kissed the top of his head.

"I'd like them to be, just let me help you. Get onto your 'intelligence' chums find out as much as you can about Sosa." There was silence then sleep.

"I need a weekend pass Mr. Jonathan, I'm down to four mill, I can handle things."

Jonathan Pritchard looked at the young man standing in front of him. He looked healthy, he'd put on weight and had been a model patient.

"Why?"

"It's to do with my last visitor and my next job."

"That doesn't sound good, your employer isn't the most altruistic of employers." Usually there's a heavy price to pay."

"Exactly, that's why I need a weekend pass, and some money."

"Can't you use your card?"

"No, they've stopped it whilst I'm here just to give me more of an incentive to complete the course as it were."

"OK. what about transport?"

"I've got a car or hadn't you noticed?"

"Of course, but no licence or insurance."

"They've taken care of that, Holman gave me the licence and they've put it on their 'special' list."

"Ok, Friday lunchtime, til Monday lunchtime, don't be late and you'll have a test as soon as you get back, test positive and you're out."

"Yes Sir." Joel mockingly saluted as he left.

Joel gently knocked and entered, she was entirely naked standing at the window looking out.

"You look like 'Gala' in the LincolnDalivision painting."

"Hello darling." Calypso didn't turn 'round.

"What are you doing?" Joel asked.

"Letting two young gardners look at me with no clothes on."

"Why?"

"I like it when men want to fuck me. Later they'll go and masterbate, not together of course." She turned around and looked at him. She didn't need to say anything she knew she was irresistibly beautiful.

"Come on, put some clothes on, let's go for a walk.

"Are you sure you want me to put some clothes on?" she moved away from the window and stood close in front of him.

"Yes, I like you to tell me what to take off next, so later." She laughed and pushed him into the chair.

"Watch me put my clothes on, just for a change. Get me some clean knickers from the second draw down."

"What colour?"

"Yellow. Where shall we walk?"

"Special place one."

"Well at least there are no graves there, that's an improvement." She tossed her head back and slipped a hair band into her hair.

"You'll need a jumper and a coat, it's not very warm out there."

"Then why are we going out in it when we could get nice and wet here."

"I need the cold to sharpen me up."

Calypso dropped to her knees in front of the concrete altar, clasped her hands in prayer, closed her eyes and said things to herself. Joel looked on from the bench.

"Are you Catholic then?" He asked as she rose.

"No, but the rest of Ireland is, I sort of got dragged along with the rituals. You may have noticed I'm not one hundred percent Irish."

"Then why did you just do that?"

"Hedging my bets I suppose, just in case."

"Come and sit with me, I want to talk to you."

"I know, you want to marry me and keep making me pregnant." She laughed as she sat as close to him as she could.

"I can help you kill Hetty Betts."

She immediately stopped, turned towards him and looked directly into his eyes.

"What are you talking about?"

"I can kill Hetty Betts for you. It's what I do. That's why I got into gear, I was in prison because of them and a friend offered me something to help, I needed it, I was a mess, it's a really complicated story but a horrible one, now they keep giving me jobs."

"Yes but Hetty Betts is my cross to bear not yours or theirs."

"I could do it as an 'extra' I have the means, they wouldn't care." Joel lied.

"Why would you do something as serious as that for me?"

"Why do you think?" Joel looked into her eyes. "Silver horses, ran down moonbeams in your dark eyes." He whispered into her ear as she kissed him.

She backed off.

"How do you know she's known as Hetty?"

"You told me, don't you remember, in the chapel in special place two." Joel lied.

"Let's go in, we'll just have time before dinner."

"I'll need you to help me do something for Constantine, he's very badly damaged, he'll never recover unless I or rather we don't help him."

"Does it entail killing someone?"

"Yes."

"And what would I have to do?"

"A honey trap, you'd be the honey."

"He may be the wrong type of bee."

"Your honey is very special ---------- honey."

"Come on, I'm cold and I need warming up. I want you to do it from behind. -- roughly, push my skirt up, pull my knickers down and don't stop til i'm wet." she took his hand and led him like a prancing stallion excited by the smell of a mare.

They lay on the soft warm bed, one spent, one satisfied.

"You were joking about Betts weren't you?"

"No. Anything you want, anything that will make you happy I'll try and give you."

She snuggled into his right armpit and stroked him.

"I'm going away in a couple of weekends."

""Have you asked my permission, How am I going to manage for a whole weekend without --- you know ----- relief?"

"Do it yourself."

"That's no fun. Where are you going?"

"Essex."

"What for?"

"See a fat slightly ginger haired woman I met on a plane going to Kathmandu who saved my life."

"What's her name?"

"Sandra."

"What does she do?"

"She's a vet, or rather will be in a couple of years."

"Why are you going to see her?"

"I need some Ketamine, or rather we do."

"What's Ketamine?"

"It's a horse anesthetic." She turned from his arm to look at him.

"Oh, of course, that answers everything." She quizzed. Shall we give dinner a miss?"

"No, if we do Trevor'll be pounding on the door and he'll see my cock when you open it."

"He won't notice it, he'll notice my tits."

"They are beautiful, maybe you're right." Joel laughed. "Come on I'm hungry."

Constantine was already seated at 'their' table. Now there were always three places set.

"Hello you two, thought you weren't going to make it, felt a bit like 'Jonny no mates'."

Calypso burst into tears as she sat down, diving into her handbag for a hanky.

"Sorry! Sorry! It's just that Constantine said a name of someone very close to me in the past. Dead now, of course but I wasn't prepared for the flood of memories, sorry what are we eating?" She wiped her face and summoned up a smile.

Connie looked at Joel.

"Well there's savoury ducks, peas, carrots, mash and gravy or steak and kidney pie, peas, carrots mash and gravy." Connie read from the small paper slipped into a green plastic holder.

"What are savoury ducks?" She directed the question without thinking to Joel.

"They're like big meat balls made of minced lamb and herbs. They're delicious, I'm going for them."

"Me too, I love big balls." She laughed and touched Joel's arm. Connie handled it well, showing no emotion.

"Have you ordered?" Joel asked Connie.

"Yes."

"I'll go over and order, what about sweet?" Calypso looked at the paper.

"I'd love apple pie and custard but I'm going to give it a miss, need to keep my figure."

"What for?" Connie asked.

Calypso thought she saw a glimmer of jealousy in his eyes, well hidden, at the back.

"A rainy day."

"We all have plenty of those." He exclaimed.

Joel got up, went over to the hatch and placed the order, the room was gently buzzing with conversations and sprinkled with occasional laughter.

"Oh, I forgot to mention, we're all going on holiday, February the second so make sure you're packed with your passports in your hands." Joel had considered how best to announce the arrangement and had decided it would be best delivered in a public arena.

"What are you talking about Joel." Connie quizzed.

"The three of us are all going on a little holiday."

"Where to?"

"Istanbul."

There was a long silence as Constantine frowned at Joel who tried not to notice. Calypso looked at Joel in amazement.

"Who's paying?"

"My friends."

"You haven't got any friends Joel -------except me." Connie added.

"I've got calypso." Joel smiled.

"She's not your friend, she's your lover, your muse, you'll do anything she wants."

"Same goes for you Connie." Joel said. The atmosphere was brittle and awkward.

"Two savoury ducks and steak and kidney" Came the shout.

The meal was difficult, not the usual light hearted banter that was the norm for their table. Calypso made an excuse and left early, muttering that she could really do with a drink. Joel looked at her arse in a very tight duck egg blue skirt as she left the room, Connie looked at Joel looking at her arse.

"What the fuck is going on Joel?" The two men looked at each other across the table.

"They want me to do a job on someone, I've told them I'll only do it after I've helped you to slay your dragon."

"How much have you told them about me?"

"Not a lot, just that something happened to you and you're not going to recover unless you redress the situation as it were."

"Have you told them what the 'something' was?"

"No of course not."

"Good, don't ever. Your lot are MI5, the workers, my lot are MI6, the managers, there's a world of difference, we recruit from Eton and Oxbridge, MI5 are usually ex police or military. One has dinner at twelve the other has lunch at one."

"I'm going to arrange it so that you can kill Sosa and his dog. Do you really want to do it?"

"That's all I want to do, it's always there in my mind, poisoning everything. I want to cut his cock and balls off and make him watch his dog eat them before I slowly kill him."

"Let's go up to your room, maybe you can forget for a short while." Joel said putting his hand on Connies.

Chapter 11.

"Hello you, I've got a weekend pass, thinking about a trip to Essex."

"Do you know where it is?"

"Somewhere near london isn't it?"

"I live in Basildon Joel, well not even Basildon, a small village outside of Basildon called Fobbing. You'll never find it."

"Your just 'Fobbing' me off cause you're living with a wavy haired stallion called Henry you met at Vet's school."

"Well I suppose 'Fobbing' you off is one up from 'wanking' you off."

"That's the reason I'm coming, I want you to do it again,--- lot's of times."

"How many times can you manage it in a weekend?"

"Don't know, six, seven, maybe eight."

"Do you think you can manage it eight times if I don't use my hand? You know, use a different part of my body?"

"I'll try my best for you Sandra, I'll try my hardest." They both laughed.

"I'll buy one of those big map books you can buy in a garage."

"Have you got a car then?"

"Well how else am I going to get to 'Fobbing'."

"Who brought it for you?"

"An exotic half negro, half Irish elite beautiful woman with incredible tits, a helicopter and an insatiable sexual appetite who likes to dominate me."

"What's her name?"

"Mr, Edenson." Joel lied. "Part of a deal, it's a green Mini with a cream roof. Can you get me two syringes full of Ketamine?"

"Ketamine's a horse anesthetic, what the fuck do you want that for?"

"And one of Lincomycin."

"That's an animal antibiotic what the fuck are you up to?"

Yes or no?"

There was a long silence.

"Yes, what time will you be here?"

"About four I guess I'll leave after lunch on Friday."

"I'll keep the bed warm."

"What about your parents?"

"They live in the farmhouse, I live in the cottage."

"Do they own a farm then?"

"Yes."

"Blimey, you know what they say about farmers' daughters?"

"What?"

"They say they're wonderful people."

"You're so full of shit Joel, see you on Friday."

"OK."

"It's not for me." Joel answered Mr. Jonathan's unspoken question as he left the office.

It was the first long journey he'd done in the Mini, it cost two and eleven to fill the small tank up. Three and tuppence with a shot of Redex. There wasn't a radio, perhaps he should get one. Joel decided he'd start collecting 'Greenshield' stamps now he was a motorist, he could get a radio with those. First target was Gloucester, then Bristol, then he'd have to look at the map again but as far as he could recall it was the A40 then the A4 all the way to London then the North Circular till the signs for Southend on Sea appeared. He'd seen on the news that there was a new bridge connecting Wales and England over the Severn estuary that cut out Gloucester but it wasn't open yet.

Being a motorist soon became tiring and boring as he stopped and started his way around the North Circular, the high state of alertness required to fend off the mobile world was draining his energy. About two o'clock after a stop at a 'Little Chef' for some pancakes, a coffee and many unscheduled stops at garages for directions. Joel sighted 'Arrowsmith Farm', well not the farm, just the entrance which hid between two lines of poplar trees and formed a single track lane with grass in the middle. The longer blades of grass were streaked with black oil. He could see a large stone farmhouse with a yellow door on the left at the end of the track and on the right was a Scandinavian style log cabin. Joel guessed that was Sandra's cottage. The small cream wheels of the Mini were no match for the track. He could hear the grass swishing underneath the car and feel the occasional tremor as the sump grazed the central hump.

Outside the log cabin was an open backed Landrover with three bales of hay chucked carelessly onto it. Beside it was a dirty dark blue Volvo Estate. 'A vets car' Joel thought to himself. He turned off the engine, put the gear stick into neutral and applied the handbrake as Calypso had taught him. Press the knob in, pull it up then release the knob. No noise!

She was wearing pale blue jeans and wellingtons. The jeans made her arse look even bigger than it was. There was no getting around it, Sandra was typical 'farming' stock, like the animals, she'd been 'bred' for the job. Her frizzy untidy gingerish hair was pulled back and tied. He looked at her. She looked wonderful, she would look after him forever.

She came toward him smiling with her lips, her eyes, her face, even her ears were smiling.

"Well you look a lot better than the last time I saw you. Look at you." She held both his hands, moving backwards so she could look him up and down. "You've put on weight. Are you off it?"

"Down to four mill a day now, another month at Bicknor and I'll be good."

"What's it like there, is it boring?"

"Not really, it's in a beautiful setting, surrounded on three sides by a river, lot's of walking, talking therapies, acupuncture, meditation, that sort of thing. The food's wonderful."

"I can see that, any friends?"

"A couple."

"Special friends?" She laughed.

"All my friends are special Sandra you know that but you are my 'special special' friend. You saved my life." Joel quickly kissed her on the nose.

"Come on let's go in, it's bloody cold, has that thing got a heater?"

"Are you referring to my wonderful car? If so the answer is yes, but I have to admit it's rather a small one."

"I prefer big ones myself." She laughed as they entered the unlocked door into an almost hot cabin. A wood burning pot belly stove creaked and spluttered away warming the wooden walls, the wooden floor and the wooden ceiling. There was only one chair, a plain wood slat back in front of an untidy large roll top desk.

"Take your coat off and sit on the bed." She said as she filled the kettle from the single tap.

"Is that all you want me to take off?"

"No. take everything off and get under the duvet."

The kettle hissed and hummed away til it boiled and clicked off as she watched him undress.

"So what's the plan?" Joel asked as she lay folded between his right arm and shoulder.

"Well I thought today we'd stay in bed, then tomorrow, we'd stay in bed, then on Sunday we'd stay in bed til you have to go."

"Well it's cheap, I'll give you that." she giggled and grabbed his spent cock.

"I have to help dad feed the cattle in about an hour then I'm done we can go to a pub tonight if you want."

"Bit scared of a pub, if I have booze I'll want a 'dig' you can always find one if you really want one, you know that."

"Why don't you have a rest whilst I finish up, I'll get a chinese take away, we'll eat it in bed then you can fuck me all night."

"Might need an aphrodisiac to keep me 'up all night'."

"How about my tits, are they big enough?" She pulled up her T-shirt over the top of her breasts, they were.

"That should do it."

Southend on Sea in November was exactly as he'd imagined. They held hands as they walked the almost deserted beach, only committed dog owners faced the biting salt wind that drove the brown dirty surf waves to destruction on the grey sand beach. No sun, no children, no dancing stars on every ripple of the sea. The pier snaked its way out towards the water.

"Do you know it's the longest pier in the world?" Sandra said as they stood together looking at it.

"Is it really? Is that why it's got a train on it?" Said Joel. "Are we going to walk up it?"

"Yes and No, I think it's shut."

"Can we have some whelks, I've never tried them?"

"OK, there's a stall further on."

"What are we going to do Joel?" Sandra asked as they walked.

"We're going to get married and live on a smallholding in Shropshire, You're going to look after the sheep, I'll look after our kids."

"Oh!"

"But I've got another job to do first for Edenson, that's why I want the Ketamine."

"How many whelks do you want?" She asked.

"Do you want any?" Joel asked.

"Yes of course, I love eating, hadn't you noticed?"

"Better get a two dozen then."

They sat in her Volvo eating Whelks in silence, letting the vinegar fight with the salt and pepper, looking at the rough sea falling over on the cold beach.

"Glad we came in your Volvo Sandra, at least it's got a big heater."

"Yes, a girl needs a big heater." They burst out into easy laughter.

She was so easy to be with, Calypso gave him a permanent hard on, If they lived together he'd have to fuck her everyday, 'then again she'd probably want more, he supposed the novelty would wear off after a while or if they made it to old age' he thought to himself. Sandra was effortless, she'd 'stimulate' him when she needed him but it wouldn't be everyday. Yes. He'd marry Sandra, people would like her at the school gate cause she wasn't a threat in the Range Rover, beauty, hair and make up, unadmitted competition that women have. He was glad he wasn't a woman.'

"What time are you leaving tomorrow?" She kicked him back to now.
"After lunch, if that's OK."
"We usually have a big family Sunday lunch in Mum and Dad's house, are you OK with that?"

They stopped on the sand.

"Meeting parents is a big thing Sandra, I'm a recovering drug addict, they'll see through me and then you'll have problems. Maybe next time if that's OK with you. I'll slip away before lunch."
"Oh! OK." Sandra's mood shifted to sombre. "You don't want to meet Mom and Dad then?"
"Not just yet, I've got this job for Edenson playing on my mind so I'm not totally relaxed. Have you got it?"
"What? The 'Special K' and Lincomycin, yes of course. That's all you came for really wasn't it?"

Joel looked into her eyes. A wisp of feisty ginger hair dangled and flapped around her full face in the wind. He kissed her very gently on the lips.

"I would have come Sandra, maybe not now, but I would have come. I have no choice. You saved my life, and now my life is yours." Sandra snuggled into his coat away from the cold wind. Joel stroked her hair.

"What If I get pregnant?" She asked as she pulled down his underpants.
"You have a baby, that's what usually happens."
"Shouldn't we use a condom?"
"I hate them, it's the smell and feel of that rubber, my cock just collapses."
"Just do it then, one more time before you go."

Chapter 12.

"Soon be Christmas." Joel commented as they walked away from the house, along the road to the gate. It was another grey, drizzly day. "Are you going to be here over Christmas?" Joel asked Calypso.

"Definitely, If I go back to Luggala all this will have been for nothing, booze will be everywhere. I feel good at the moment, you know, strong and clean. What about you?"

"The same as you, I could go to my friend Sandra's place in Essex but booze will weaken my resolve and I'll be fucked. Alcohol's the biggest cause of relapse into gear, did you know that?"

"No, but it makes sense. Shall we walk down to the village for a hot pie from the Post Office."

"Sounds good."

From the cattle grid onwards it got dark. The hill and its dense trees on the left, less trees on the right. The ground dropped away steeply on the right changing into gardens and steep driveways for dotted shadowed houses. The road meandered downwards, there were cracks in the tarmac where eventually the surface would give way and collapse down the hill but for now it was OK, just bending and blending with the curves.

"Tell me more about this exotic trip you're taking me on."

"Well Edenson wants me to do a job, I've told him I won't do it unless I help Connie get better first. I'm pushing it a bit, for two pins they'd just get rid of me."

"Rubbish, they've spent too much money on you. You've got something they need."

"Suppose you're right, anyway Edenson's going along with it. He thinks it's just a break weekend in Istanbul, a jolly to cheer up Constantine. Apparently MI5 don't talk too much to MI6 or they'd have put two and two together by now."

"This sounds awfully serious darling."

A very steep track on the right led to some cottages and then down to t
railway bridge. A nearby railway tunnel entrance was shuttered off but curious hik.
and brave children had found a way in. Two hundred yards down the track was an
old landrover used as a four wheel drive escape vehicle during bad weather.
Bounding up the track as though it was descending rather than steeply ascending
came a large, almost black Rottweiler the skin around it's open barking jaws, bright
red and very wet, it's black piglike eyes set wide on its head targeted Joel and
Calypso. Joel spotted the dog a second before Calypso. He froze as the fast moving
heavy animal closed in on them. Snarling, growling with curled back skin
unsheathing dagger teeth. Calypso finally realised, turned towards the dog and
looked at it. The dog stopped in it's tracks, lowered it's head and slunk off, almost
whimpering before disappearing from view down the track.

"How on earth did you do that?" He asked.
"Do what?"
"Send that dog packing. I was all set to run but decided against it as it would
have been a lot faster than me."
"Don't know, it's just something that's in me, something in my past I suppose.
I've always had this power over animals, suppose it's the same with lots of women
and horses."
"Do you think you could do it with a huge Afghan Kuchi dog."
"No idea what they look like but yes, I can control most animals."
"Do you think that comes from your African Negro roots, you know the jungle
and all that?"
"Is it that obvious?"
"What?"
"My mixed race, my genes?"
"No." Joel lied. But your Jeans look very nice from here." He laughed,
obviously staring at her arse. "Bet you'd look incredible in really tight very short
denim shorts and really high stilettos."
"I'd look 'tarty'."
"I love 'tarts'. They give me an instant hard on every time I see one."
"I'll buy some shorts." She laughed.
"Suppose I've got to buy the pies now you've saved me from being mauled to
death by a crazed Rottweiler."
"Yes of course." She laughed and tucked herself into his arm.

They ate their hot steak and kidney pies in the cold air, leaning on the old
stone parapet of the bridge watching the occasional car go underneath.

"Tell me seriously what the plan is for Istanbul?" Calypso said between
mouthfuls.

tantine was working for the intelligence services, MI6 in Istanbul, trying
important Russian defector. Philby was there at the time, in fact he was
s, nobody knew at the time he was a Russian spy, had been all his life."
ς Philby?"

Joel looked up in mock dismay from his steaming pie.

"Kim Philby? The Cambridge five? Cairncross, MaClean, Burgess and Blunt?
Ringing any bells?"

*not known until years
late,
79ɔ90*

"Sorry no."
"God! Where've you been the last few years?"
"In a gilded cage getting pissed."
"Sorry, sorry, bit crass of me that." Joel touched her hand.
"Go on."
"Well Philby must have passed information to the Russians who passed it
onto the Turks. Anyway come the day of the defection Connie got arrested, it was a
sting operation, the Russians and Turks knew every detail. They did horrible things
to Connie before he managed to get away. He's lucky to be alive.
"So why do you care?" Calypso lowered her pie and looked into him.

Joel took a long time to answer.

"I think I love him?"
"As well as me?"

There was no hesitancy.

"Yes."
"As well as Sandra?"
"Yes, but all differently."

Calypso and Joel leant on the stones, finishing their pies and looking at the
river curving away in the distance.

"Come on I'm getting cold, let's go back and warm up in bed."
"OK." Joel said, taking her silver foil pie tray and paper bag, screwing them up
with his own and putting them in his pocket. They set off up the hill in silence holding
hands.

"Is that 'tarty' enough for you?" She wore high heels, tiny cream lace knickers
that hid nothing and nothing else as she sashayed from the bathroom towards the
bed, her breasts moving a fraction of a second after her body. "Have you got a hard
on?" She held up her breasts towards him with her hands.

"Yes."
"Let me check? Show me!" she commanded.

Joel pulled back the duvet.
"Seems to be OK." She climbed over him and moaned as two became one.

Afterwards she lay warm, safe and sober in his arms.

"So what is it exactly you want me to do?"

"Lure Captain Sosa to a hotel room."
"I wont actually have to fuck him will I?"
"No, that's not in the plan. You will probably have to deal with his dog though. It never leaves his side."
"And how do I get to meet this 'Captain'?"
"Connie or rather Connie's colleagues will organise a reception at the Embassy to which he will be invited."
"Will they invite his dog?"
"Not specifically but he'll come anyway he'll be with his car and driver outside."
"Sounds fun, what if he's handsome with a large oriental one, you know, one of those that curves upwards, you see them in naughty little brass figurines they sell in hippy shops."
"Well I suppose you could consider it a farewell treat.."
"Are we lunching?"
"I'm not, I'm full after that pie."
"I'm full as well." She put her hand around his balls and giggled.
"Anything left in these?"
"No idea, suck it and find out."
"Do you want to watch me?"
"Yes."

Whatever Calypso did to him was intense, he could never last long with her. Afterwards, smiling with mischief she kissed him, forcing her tongue into his mouth. Sharing everything.

"How exactly are you going to dispose of horrible Hetty Betts?"
"I've got a secret weapon."
"Yes I know, and I love it."

Joel kicked her under the duvet.

"I thought it was a serious question."
"It is, 'deadly' serious."

"Edenson, or rather his boss Holman has given me an umbrella."

"You're going to kill Hetty Betts for me, cause you love me, with an umbrella?"

"Yes. I've got two of them. " Joel lied, "One for the job they want me to do and a spare should it malfunction. I'll use the spare for Ms Betts."

"What do you do, beat them to death with the handle or turn it upside down, collect some rain and drown them?"

"Neither. Got to go now, got a counselling session at two." Joel got out of bed and made for his discarded clothes on the chair.

"Bring your underpants here I want to put them on for you."

"Joel stood still as she knelt down and slowly eased his pants up his legs til she slowly covered him up.

"Do they help?" She asked.

"What?"

"The counselling sessions?"

"Don't really know, but they do make you ask questions about yourself."

"Oh God, I couldn't cope with that."

"What about yours?"

"Coping mechanisms really, how to manage the now and forever, quite useful really."

Joel kissed her on the nose and left.

"There's a registered envelope for you in my office, it's your plane tickets." Jonathan said as they passed in the large round hall.

"You've opened it then?"

"Yes of course, there might have been prohibited substances in it. Business Class, how on earth did you manage that for your exotic break?"

"Contacts in high places."

"Thought you'd been visiting the church a lot."

"Is there anything you miss?" Joel asked.

"Not a lot, the medics tell me you're clear now, well done, remember it takes about two years to really feel better. Will you be coming back after your 'holiday'?"

"Probably just to say goodbye and collect my things if all goes well."

"And if it doesn't?"

"I won't be back." Jonathan stood back and looked at him.

"Bit of a waste if I lose three of my successes at one go so to speak."

"Better keep your fingers crossed then."

Jonathan and Joel entered the large light airy office for the envelope.

It was dinnertime. Joel sat on Connie's bed waiting for him to come out of the bathroom.

"I have the tickets for Istanbul." Joel shouted to him.

"You mean Constantinople, don't you?" The voice floated out of the open door. "They named it after me you know."

"Yes OK. It says on the tickets 'Istanbul'."

"Obviously a mistake, when is it we go? Remind me."

"February the second."

Constantine Ellis emerged from the bathroom clean and shiny but fully clothed.

"Have you told Calypso yet?"

"Not yet, I'll tell her at dinner."

"Are you sure she'll do this for us, for me, for you?"

"Yes, she loves my cock and I'm attached to it."

"So do I." Connie laughed. "Come on let's go down."

"Bad choice of words after your last comment." Joel retorted.

Calypso was there before them. She looked lovely, they both thought so, they both said so. She wore an almost see through subtly floral peachy pink blouse, a very pale turquoise skirt and the merest hint of make up around her eyes.

"Ok, we're on, I've got the tickets for Istanbul, leave ten fifteen Wednesday the second of Feb, come back ten days later." Joel gave Calypso her ticket.

"You keep it for me darling I'll only lose it." She smiled and touched his hand.

"Same with me Joel, you keep them."

"Take it you've both got your passports with you?"

Constantine and Calypso nodded.

"What are we eating?" Connie asked. "I'm for the poached salmon and new potatoes."

"Liver and onions for me." Joel fingered the green plastic menu holder.

"I'm with Constantine today darling, poached salmon."

"I'll go and order then." Joel got up and moved towards the kitchen hatch.

"This is not going to be nice, you realise that Calypso don't you?"

She looked directly at Constantine.

"What, the poached salmon or Istanbul?"

"I'm going to kill a man, as nastily and cruelly as I possibly can."

"Well at least it's better than doing nothing, which is what I do." She lowered her long eyelashes at him.

Joel returned.

"Business Class, how on earth did you wangle that one Joel?" Connie asked, sipping at his glass of water.
"Bonus from Edenson."
"I somehow doubt that, they must rate you Joel."
"I've been lucky my last two jobs for them turned out OK."
"Do you like my blouse?" Calypso asked. "It's a Balenciaga."

"Mr Joel, two salmons and one liver." The unseen voice rang out from the other side of the hatch.

"That's us then." Connie said as all three of them got up.
"Yes I do, the colour is perfect for you." Joel whispered as they walked over to the hatch. He could see the eyes of other men in the room irresistibly following her.

The food, as always, was delicious.

"So, what's on the agenda tomorrow?" Connie asked, wiping his mouth with a serviette.
"Well I've got Mrs Pemberton for a therapy session." Calypso replied. " last time we discussed hormones and decided that men's body odour and smelly feet were in direct correlation to their sex drives as boys feet don't stink, neither do old mens feet, neither do they have to use underarm deodorants but sexually active men always smell."
"You're quite right calypso, I have no need for deodorants and my socks are virtually sterile." Connie sarcastically said.
"Mine aren't" Joel chirped in then instantly regretted it as he looked at Constantine.
"Looks like you and me for a walk tomorrow morning then Joel. Don't forget to wear clean socks and wash under your arms." Connie said with a smile. Joel felt forgiven.

It was an on off rainy day, the wind provided the on off, the clouds provided the rain. It was ten when Joel and Constantine closed the door on the resilient yellow mansion, it was though the rain was just a minor irritant to the centuries old house.

"Where to?" Connie asked.
"Let's go and look at the old church on the river bank, been passed it loads of times but never bothered to go in it."
"OK but we'll need waterproofs."

The decaying concrete track was rough, rising in places as tree roots inexorably pushed up, sinking away in other places as it gave way to gravity, just pot holed everywhere as water constantly attacked. It snaked down past the pale stone youth hostel then spilled exhausted onto the wide grass bank that bordered the river. Trees bordered everything, an old stone wall bordered the small graveyard that surrounded the church. Joel and Constantine stood silently together under the slated timber lychgate.

"I wonder who the last people to get married in this magical place were?" Constantine muttered quietly.

"No idea but I expect it was a man and woman."

"What? You mean the vicar wouldn't be too keen to marry you and I even if I told him we were in love and I was a fucking eunuch." Connie was almost crying.

"Is that true Connie?"

"Of course it's true, I've got no balls."

"No. You know what I mean. Are we in love?"

"I am, how about you?" Connie looked at him as he asked the question.

"I think so."

"With Calypso?"

"Yes."

"With Sandra?"

"Yes."

"What about me?"

"Yes, shall we go and look inside?"

The stalwart stone square tower stood on the right of the door. It was almost a sentry, silently shouting, 'Halt! Who goes there!' It still smelt damp from last year's flood. But the inside was peaceful in its age old simple beauty. There were flowers in vases, the old oak pews were polished and shiny. Like all churches, it demanded subservient quiet respect. Constantine knelt on a pew to pray. His prayer was silent. He got up and glanced at Joel.

"Do you believe then?" Joel asked.

"Yes and no, I suppose it's a bit like insurance, you could risk it and take a chance without any but you feel so much better with it. Somedays I question 'why me' then the next day I conclude 'why not me?' You?"

"I've done bad things, when it's him or me, it's always me, so I don't feel worthy enough to even consider it."

"Come on sit down next to me. Hold my hand, it makes me feel safe."

Joel sat down on the pew alongside Connie and held his hand.

"What are your plans regarding Sosa?" Connie asked.

"I've got two syringes full of Ketamine and one full of Lincomycin. You need to arrange an important reception at the Embassy. Sosa will be invited along with others from the Turkish diplomatic service. Calypso will captivate him and take him back to her hotel room, when he's 'otherwise engaged' as it were, we'll go into the room. I suggest a Stanley knife."

"What will Ketamine do?"

"He won't be able to move, conscious but paralysed, it's called going into a 'K-hole', never experienced it myself, thank god."

"Sounds perfect, What's the other stuff for?"

"Lincomycin, it will be in a special hair pin that Calypso will stab him with when he's 'excited' so to speak. That will temporarily incapacitate him whilst we go in and inject the 'Special K', then we're going to leave you to it, the second syringe is for the dog."

"Is she going to fuck him?"

"Not sure, I expect she will, especially if he's got a big cock."

"What about the dog?"

"It will be in the room, Calypso will control it, she has this strange power over animals."

"My intention is to cut off Sosa's cock and balls and feed them to his fucking dog, then watch him bleed to death." Connie stared at the Altar as he said the words.

"Are you going to kill the dog as well?"

"Yes, I want Sosa to watch me kill it so he'll know he's next"

Joel squoze his hand.

"Remind me never to get on the wrong side of you. What prayer did you say when you came in here?"

Connie looked at Joel.

"I prayed for you and I to be safe and happy."

"Was that safe and happy 'together'?"

"Come on It's chilly in here, it's always cold in churches have you noticed?"

"I need another device." Joel spoke quietly, almost a whisper into the phone, not wanting Jonathan to hear.

"What? You've broken or fired off the umbrella?" Edenson was his usual brusque self, no 'hello' or social niceties.

"No, it's not an umbrella, I need a lady's hair pin that's really a syringe, long, slim and sharp, with some sort of fake jewel on the top which you press and it pumps out the stuff."

"What stuff?"

"Lincomycin, do you want Betts dead, yes or no?"

"I'll talk to the department." The phone went dead.

It was early January, persistent white dust snow lingered on the ground. Pheasants, glorious in their red brown winter plumage were confident and raucous as they posed in the snow.

"Mr. Edenson is coming to see you tomorrow morning Joel so don't disappear." Jonathan informed him as he headed out with Calypso. "I expect it will be his last visit seeing as you're clear now."

"Ok, what time?"

"He didn't say but it's usually about ten, ten thirty, in time for morning coffee."

Calypso pulled on his gloved finger and tugged him towards the door.

"Come on darling, I feel the need for something long, meaty and hot." She purposely said it loudly for Jonathan to hear.

"A sausage roll at the village Post Office then is it Ms Calypso?" Jonathan joined in the game.

"Of course." She giggled.

It was a 'teal' blue Rover three litre coupe that almost glided silently up to the front splay of Bicknor Court. 'Edenson looked even more shiny than usual' Joel thought to himself as he looked out of the dining room window. Constantine was with him, sharing morning coffee with 'Arrowroot' biscuits.

"Here's my nemesis."

"That's a bit severe, he's just a Civil Servant."

"Civil Servant my arse, they run the fucking country. Him and people like him, nobody came recruiting for the Diplomatic Service in 'Happy Valley'."

"Where's that?"

"It's a hippy commune in darkest wettest Wales. It's the only place my mother wanted to live."

"Wanted or could afford?" Constantine asked.

"Both."

"You don't like him then?"

"Well just look at him, Gleaming black leather shoes that aren't patent leather but actually spit and polished. Must take him hours to do that, Dark blue Saville Row suit, that probably cost more than the average working man's yearly wage, cream cotton shirt and expensive lilac silk tie. His Brief case probably cost more than all my clothes."

"That's how I dressed when I was working at the Embassy."

Joel put his cup down slowly onto the bone china saucer and looked at Constantine.

"Yes but you're incredibly brave and intelligent, he's just incredibly privileged and probably hates travelling out of London, plus I don't love him."

"Put your best smile on and go and greet him, I'll wait in my room for you. Where's Calypso this morning?"

"Resting in bed, it's her 'inconvenient time' as she describes it, think she suffers badly from it."

"Oh! Glad I'm just a eunuch and not a woman."

"Stop saying that. You'll depress yourself."

"What? Even more! Impossible."

"Good morning Mr. Edenson, good trip?"

It was a good morning, a late November morning, clear and bright, the hoar frost lingering on everything in a shadow. Late shedding trees with dangling dead leaves craved the weak sun to turn them with the breeze, till they dropped discarded from the bow. *bough*

"Morning Mr.Joel, you look well."

"I am well."

"Good. Where can we talk?"

"In the dining room if you like, there's usually no one there this time of day and you can have a coffee."

"Any cakes?"

Joel looked at Edenson. Yes, he looked the kind of man that liked cakes, he looked big but actually he wasn't, he was small framed with quite a lot of fat. His face was round and congenial but somehow the eyes didn't go with the smile.

"Sorry, just plain biscuits I'm afraid, we only have cakes when it's someone's birthday."

Edenson looked disappointed.

"Tell me Mr. Joel I'm intrigued by your request for tickets, first it was to be two tickets to Hong Kong, then it changed to three tickets to Istanbul."

There was a silence as Joel poured out the coffee.

"I need someone's help to get close to Betts. By total coincidence and I must say an amazing coincidence, there's a woman here who knows her as a friend but what Betts doesn't know is she, - the woman - blames Betts for the death of her husband, an RAF pilot called Jolyon Clay and her lover another RAF pilot called Jonny Conrad. There's some mystery over her husbands jet fighter disappearing and Conrad committed suicide probably because of Clays death. Apparently they were best friends to the extent that Conrad was best man at their wedding. Anyway she's convinced Betts manipulated her husband's socialist sympathies to the extent that it caused his death. The file you gave me backs up her story."

"What's her name?"

"Calypso Clay is her married name but her maiden name was Calypso Fortnum-Guinness from Southern Ireland, so draw your own conclusions about that. She has a son by her late husband called Salvador, he's heir to the estate when he comes of age which is in about six or seven years' time. Calypso herself is half negro, a transgression by her mother on a Caribbean Island during their honeymoon. She's barely tolerated within the family so she turned to booze, hence she's here."

"So where do the tickets and Istanbul come in?"

"She's in love with a diplomat that's here, a chap called Constantine Ellis, he had a really bad time in Istanbul when he was trying to recruit a high ranking Russian called Volkod, it was the time when Philby was head of station for MI6 in Istanbul and everything was going back to Moscow who passed it onto the Turks to deal with. Ellis got arrested and badly tortured, so badly that he's not quite a man any more if you get my drift, anyway Calypso has vowed to help Constantine kill a Captain Sosa and his huge dog, They both work for the Turkish MIT but the dog never draws his salary." Joel joked but Edenson didn't laugh. "Surely you know all this, you're part of the intelligence service?"

"They're MI6 Mr. Joel, the Eton, Oxbridge lot, the 'Old School Tie' brigade, pink gins on the veranda, everything done with a nod and a wink."

"And what are you Mr. Edenson?"

"MI5, we're the real workers, we keep the country safe, just look what happened with the Cambridge five, all communists in their youth but still allowed into key security positions because of elitism."

It was the first time Edenson had opened up on anything.

"Go on Mr. Joel."

"That's it, I have to help her, or them, kill Sosa and his dog then she will help me get close to Betts. She will think it's for her, because all three of us are friends but as we both know it's for us, I use that term very loosely Mr. Edenson."

"Does she know that Betts is your target?"

"Course not."

Edenson was silent.

"So! Let me get this straight, in order for her helping you to kill someone she hates, she wants you to help kill her lover's Nemesis?"

"And his dog."

"And what do you want out of this?"

"A smallholding in Shropshire, something between Ludlow and Shrewsbury."

"A smallholding in Shropshire."

"Yes."

"How many acres?"

"No more than fifty."

Edenson looked incredulous as he sipped his coffee. Without thinking he dunked his arrowroot."

universities

"You're right, you're not Oxbridge are you Mr. Edenson?"

school "Charterhouse. Why the smallholding?"

"I'm going to get married?"

"Who to?"

"A vet."

"Does she know, I'm presuming it's a she."

"No, not yet, and your presumption is correct."

"The sooner the better on Betts, don't want any more expensive defections or love torn suicides. Or for that matter any more disruptive demonstrations at Holylock."

"Soon as I can Mr. Edenson, soon as I can. Have you got it?"

"Got what?"

"The hair pin, hat pin, whatever it is."

"Oh yes."

Edenson reached down into his briefcase and produced what looked like a dark blue fountain pen box.

"Now, to fill it just unscrew the jewelled top, usual left hand thread, nothing too complicated. You fill it with whatever with a syringe. It's telescopic and very sharp so be careful, once it's in, just press the end down and bob's your uncle. You can only use it once as there's a diaphragm seal in the barrel, once that's ruptured it's no good. It's single use only so be very careful with it."

"Thanks, I will."

Edenson's driver never got out of the car. Calypso watched from her bedroom window. Her thoughts skipping over the stunted winter grass of the gently descending dull green fields to Salvador. She desperately wanted to see him, to be with him, to hug him, to kiss him. He would be at Bovington for Christmas, the Clays always did a good Christmas, huge tree in the galleried hall. She could just leave, go there now, pack her bags and go, it wasn't a prison, she was there voluntarily and paying a small fortune for it. She looked at Joel as he saw off Mr. Civil Servant in his comfortable Rover. God he was handsome, younger than her, probably the last real passion she'd have in her life. He was one reason to stay, the other was the booze at Christmas, it was everywhere, offered at every occasion, every meeting, every meal, even offered to Father Christmas on a plate by the tree with a mince pie, a carrot and bowl of water. He wasn't real but the booze was, it was taking a long time for it to become insignificant in her life, Joel helped, Bicknor Court helped but she couldn't rely on herself just yet. She needed support and a cause, here she had both.

"Hello you." She looked into his eyes forever.
"Hello." Have you missed me?" Joel asked.
"Terribly. Everything OK?"
"Yes, get Christmas and New Year over and we're bound for Istanbul or rather Constantinople. Connie insists they named it after him."
"He would, he's a member of the ruling elite, they think the whole world revolves around them, and London is the capital of the world."
"It is, isn't it?" Joel laughed.

Calypso dug him in the ribs with her right elbow.
"Upstairs to my room now! Go into my bathroom and wait till I call you out."

After five minutes she called out. She stood there in just ridiculously high heels and the shortest briefest tightest denim shorts he had ever seen. Slowly she turned around laughing and giggling letting him stare at her bottom before teetering over to stand in front of him and unzipping him.

"You weren't lying were you, tarts really do give you a very big hard on."
"I don't think there's any room for knickers under those shorts." Joel commented.
"There isn't."

About seventy five percent of Bicknor Court had gone home for Christmas. It was New Years Eve, the Christmas cards on the mantelpiece above the huge marble clad fireplace in the lounge were looking tired, curling and bending with fatigue. Calypso and Joel sat together on the large sofa staring at the fire and throwing discarded horse chestnut shells into it. Mr. Jonathan and Constantine were seated in the two armchairs. Mr. Jonathan reading a National Geographic magazine and nibbling on pistachios, Constantine half asleep, half watching the TV which flickered away in the corner of the large room. The TV was showing a rerun of last year's firework display in Edinburgh. Joel reached into the big wicker basket and chose the biggest log to carefully place on the open fire. Calypso quickly resumed her former position, snuggled up toJoel with her knees curled up on the sofa. They watched the new log start to pop and spit, little jets of smoky steam coming out of it.

Sweet

"Come on let's go and walk along the Embankment."

Everyone turned to look at Jonathan.

"What do you mean?" Asked Joel.
"I mean let's all get in my Citroen and go down to the Embankment in London to see if there are any drunken revellers crazy enough to be out and about on a cold black night."
"It's two and and a half to three hours to London Mr. Jonathan." Constantine had been jolted from his lethargy by the totally unexpected uncharacteristic suggestion by the manager.
"It's only seven o'clock, if we get a move on we could be there for eleven. Anybody know their way around London?"

There was a short silence.

"I do, my club, 'The Livery' is close to the Embankment." Constantine said.

"Let's go then!" Joel slapped Calypso's knee as he got up."
"Are you serious Mr. Jonathan?" He asked.
"Of course, can't think of anything more excruciatingly boring than seeing in the New Year watching Andy Stewart in his kilt on the TV with you lot."

in 66?

The big Citroen DS Estate swallowed them all up with comfortable ease as it cruised towards Gloucester. The roads were virtually empty. Jonathan put an Andy Williams Christmas song compilation into his new radio / cassette player, it seemed to reflect the progress of the car, smooth and effortless. It was mainly silent, everyone deep into their own thoughts, their own world. Calypso and Joel had to touch each other, their legs pressed together on the seat. Joel wrestled with his feelings, she was so beautiful, so sexy, but he knew she would be trouble, expensive and trouble, beautiful women always were. All other men would be suspect, you could never just have a friend, you'd always be wondering. No, Sandra would be far safer, she'd always be there for him. Calypso was like a star, brilliant but always moving, Sandra was Mount Everest, immovable and eternal. Then there was Constantine? He almost felt he should always be there for him, looking after him, seeing him through his current predicament to the other side, till he found his own way again, found someone else to love.

It was like something from an old black and white film but there was no swirling smog. The stout black ornamental stanchions almost invisible till the round globe light at the top exposed them. The leafless trees immune to the wind and cold, retracted and safe within their slender branches, waiting patiently for light and warmth. Calypso huddled into Joel. Constantine and Jonathan walked side by side chatting as they all headed slowly up towards Big Ben. A small crowd of drunken revellers gathered just before the steps leading up to the bridge. All eyes were on the big hand of the clock as it edged towards twelve. It seemed reluctant to edge forward into the new year.

The familiar chimes followed by twelve 'Bongs' rang out, everybody cheered, hugged and kissed.

"Nineteen Sixty Six, I wonder where that will take us?" Calypso said disengaging from a long sensual kiss.
"Istanbul." Joel replied.

Constantine broke away from Jonathan, kissed Calypso on the cheek then hugged Joel tightly for a long time.
"Happy New Year my handsome prince." He kissed him quickly but on the lips, making sure Calypso could hear and see. Staking his claim to possession.

Jonathan held back then shook everyone's hand.

"Well let's hope for a peaceful and healthy year." He said to everyone.
"Not much chance of 'peaceful' with Vietnam kicking off but we might make it with 'healthy'." Joel laughed, putting his arms around the shoulders of Constantine and Calypso as they turned to walk away from Big Ben towards Waterloo.

"I'm hungry." Said Connie.
"What about your Club?" Joel asked.
"Good lord no, anyway it's a 'Gentlemens' club and Calypso's a woman, haven't you noticed?"
"Now you come to mention it, there is something different about her." They all laughed.
"There's bound to be a hot dog van or something by Waterloo Bridge." Jonathan said.
"That sounds wonderful, lots of onions and mustard." Joel said.
"I've never had one, are they nice?" Calypso said.
"You're joking?" Connie commented.
"No, why would I eat food from a van?" Calypso responded.
"Errr because it's delicious."Joel nudged her with his elbow.
"OK, I'll risk it. Who's paying?"
"Mr. Jonathan." They all chorussed.

Jonathan drove the quiet Citroen in silence as everyone fell asleep. Calypso with her head on Joel's lap, Constantine with his head on Joel's shoulder. No one sat in the front passenger seat. It was four fifteen in the morning before the car came to a sedate halt in front of Bicknor Court.

Chapter 13.

Looking back over his shoulder the pale yellow safety of Bicknor Court slowly got smaller as Jonathan's Citroen gently cruised through the gate and over the cattle grid. The big wheels, fluid suspension and compliant tyres barely revealed they were travelling over bars of iron. It was early in the morning, still dark but you could sense dawn would reveal another dull grey cold day. The heater warmed the inside quickly. Calypso snuggled up to Joel, Constantine was in the front passenger seat. Their luggage was piled in the back. The road towards Bristol ran alongside the tidal River Avon as it pushed it's way inland. Steep shiny mud buttresses contained what seemed like a trickling stream, only to become a navigable river when the moon let it. Through a tunnel then under Mr. Brunel's famous bridge spanning the gorge way above them, then turn right for the airport.

"What hotel are we in?" Calypso asked as they descended the steps to the cold concrete of Yesilkoy airport. It was a short chilly walk of about three hundred yards to the warmth of the terminal.

"We haven't actually got one yet. Constantine says the Bosphorus is good and it's close to the Embassy." Joel replied.

"Actually I'll be staying at the Embassy itself. I'm still a MI6 Officer so as a casual visitor I get a room in the Embassy. It'll give me a chance to re-establish myself with the staff and smooze them into arranging the reception. I know the Ambassador so it shouldn't be too difficult."

"How are you going to justify the reception? You can hardly say to set a trap for Captain Sosa and then kill him."

"I'll just say it's to re-establish old friendships and contacts prior to me starting work again. They'll re badge that into something like a reception to welcome a new senior member of staff or somebody leaving. Spying is all about friendships and relationships, nothing is professional, everything is personal."

"So they think this visit is official then?" Joel enquired.

"Let's put it this way, I haven't told them that it's not."

"And are you going to work here again?"

"Not if i can help it. Not too keen on Turkish food, lots of lamb, grease and sweets. Might try for somewhere like Cairo or Riyadh."

"Wouldn't that be the same? They're Arabs you know."

"Probably, but at least there wouldn't be any nasty memories and I do like the heat."

"Will you come with us to the hotel? Help us find our feet as it were, we're both innocent tourists in a new town."

"Of course. Will you want one or two rooms?"

There was an awkward moment, an unsure silence. Joel looked at Calypso but didn't want to hurt Constantine even though he knew full well that they were lovers.

"Better have two, one for work, one for play." Calypso assertively replied. "I hope the bed's really big in the 'playroom'." She glanced mischievously at Joel.

The taxi was old, big, American and black. Constantine, Joel and Calypso squashed together on the bench back seat. The driver seemed too small for such a big car.

"How do you feel Connie?" Joel asked as they headed through the ancient streets.

"I have to admit, somewhat nervous, my memories are not particularly pleasant, in fact when I flew out of here I never wanted to come back - ever! Yet here I am."

"It's a bit like falling off a horse, apparently unless you get straight back on, taking that you've not broken anything , you'll never ride again." Calypso commented, her attention glued to the passing alien scenes that were flashing by, some quickly, some slowly. "I suspect Constantine, that unless you bury this ghost you won't be able to move on, you know, get your life back."

"End one to start one then?" Connie commented.

"Exactly, shame about the dog though."

"The dog's just an extension of an evil man, it's got to go."

"Here we are, Bosphorus Palace Hotel, looks OK." Joel deliberately interrupted.

"I won't come in with you if you don't mind, they'll have cameras and I'm shy."

"OK, see you tomorrow then, what time?" Joel asked,

"How about two-ish tomorrow afternoon? I'll show you a few sights."

"Can't wait." Calypso sarcastically replied.

Joel's room had three tall windows with dark reddish brocade heavy curtains, pale lilac walls with dull gold embellishments. The bed was huge with matching bronze coloured bedding. Calypso immediately threw herself backwards onto it.

"Seems OK, shall we try it out? I've been desperate for your cock all day."
"Oh well, in that case!"

Calypso shouted from the shower.

"What are you doing?"
"Reading all the tourist stuff."
"And?"
"The Hagia Sophia is a must visit."
"What is it?"
"Well, originally it was an orthodox Christian Cathedral, that was about one thousand five hundred years ago mind, then it became a Catholic Cathedral, then during the Ottoman Empire it became a Mosque and now it's a museum."
Calypso came out of the bathroom dripping with water and nothing else, she carried a large soft hotel towel.

"Dry me." She flung the towel playfully at Joel. "Dry me slowly and tell me what else we're going to do."
"The blue mosque."
"That sounds Islamic, can I go in it?"
"Of course but I can't wear shorts and you need a headscarf or something to cover your head. Apparently the hand painted mosaics are amazing, it's about four hundred years old and is bathed in blue lights at night. Or so it says here."
"And?"
"You're very wet here, do you want me to dry it some more?"
"Yes please."
"The Topkapi Palace Museum."
"Sounds boring."
"The Sultans of the Ottoman Empire used to live in it and kept a harem of women in it."
"Oooh I'd love that, just kept to be fucked, no matter if I got pregnant or not, just kept for sex, i could live with that. No pretence, no consideration, just like the monkeys in the jungle. He'd wake up, fuck me then go off for breakfast. Then he'd go and fuck somebody else and I could be all jealous and bitchy."
"I could fuck you then we could go down for dinner."
"Go down on me, then fuck me very hard and quick, don't care about my feelings just do it til you come and I'll pretend I'm your concubine. Then we'll go down for dinner."

"There was a film called Topkapi, I vaguely remember seeing it when I was a teenager. I remember someone dangling upside down inside it trying to steal a dagger with a famous jewel on it. Melinda, no, Melina Mercouri was the star."

"Was she as beautiful as me?"

"Of course not."

"Right answer."

"Apparently Captain Sosa is a Major now, still with MIT, still with his dog, still killing people." Constantine said as they got into a taxi. "Don't forget to put your clothes and stuff in 'your' room Calypso. Sosa's smart, if things don't add up he'll run a mile. The Ambassador has agreed to a reception on the eighth, we fly home on the twelfth, I wanted it a couple of days later, ideally the tenth but that just wasn't possible with the Embassy calendar. Where are we going?"

"Topkapi Palace, Calypso wants to do it hanging upside down." Joel laughed.

"There's a secret door you know."

"Where?" Calypso asked.

"In the Imperial Hall, there are three mirrors, the centre mirror is really a secret door, you can't tell, it's so good."

"Where does it lead to?" Joel asked.

"Just a balcony I think, I've seen it but never been through it, I don't think they allow anyone to go through it. It's a secret."

"How do you know about it?"

"Philby told me, he loves secrets, that was his 'raison d'etre' as it were, knowing something you didn't. I suppose that was why he was a spy, the excitement of it, living on the edge, deceiving everybody, his wife, his kids, his bosses, everybody."

The entrance was a triple affair, light grey stone set in beige, almost pink stone walls. A tall arched tunnel entry was guarded by two similar but smaller arched alcoves either side. Constantine paid the taxi as they joined the small clutch of queueing tourists.

"Any progress with the reception?" Joel asked.

"Yes, all organised, seven thirty for eight on the eighth. It's to welcome the new deputy Ambassador, it really is, just a convenient coincidence."

"And Sosa has been invited?"

"Well, not by name, it's usual just to send out a number of invitations. Four have been sent to MIT. He won't be able to resist it, an evening schmoozing with the British Diplomatic Service, a chance to recruit or at least look for possibles. No he'll be there alright. What are you going to wear Calypso?"

"long or short?" She asked.

"Long really stylish, short at a push."

"I've brought a light blue calf length Versace, will that do?"

"Does it show your breasts off?" Connie asked.

"Yes, very well."

"That will do. Wow, just look at that!" Constantine, Joel and Calypso just stood still and stared into the Imperial Throne Room. Muted reds and blues arched above as they gave way to gold. The light of the day changed the splendour as they moved around.

Joel's fingers brushed against Calypso's as they moved within the magnificent room. Then she was holding his finger. It was as though she was a little girl with an ice cream. They all stared at the opulent magnificence of the ancient room.

"I want to wear very loose silk 'harem' pants with no knickers, you know, so loose they almost fall down by themselves with just the mearest knotted see through top to hold my breasts up so the Sultan will notice them and choose me to fuck."

"What about your Yashmak?" Constantine asked.

"Gossamer thin lilac silk, with a jewel encrusted comb to hold my hair back as it swayed to the music."

"You've obviously missed your vocation Calypso." He responded.

The coffee was small black and sweet, there was no option, that's the way it was. The large white parasols gently moved in the breeze. The blue of the Bosphorus could just be seen. A large plate of Lokum, some with dates, some with hazelnuts accompanied the coffee. There was an easy relaxed silence as everyone relaxed into the wicker chairs.

"What's it like Connie?"

"What's what like?"

"Living in an Embassy." Joel asked.

"Like living in a 'Gentlemans club' a maze of unwritten, unspoken rules that everyone knows and obeys. If you break them, or don't know them, you're not part of the club."

"Absolute ruthlessness in the most subtle way." Calypso replied.

"How on earth would you know that?" Joel asked.

"Cause that's how the English work. I'm part Jamaican, part Irish I've seen how it works, experienced it. Salvador is part of the club, I'm not, I'm just the vehicle he arrived in."

"That's a bit severe." Joel commented.

"It's true, she's right." Constantine concurred.

"So what's the plan for tomorrow? Run it passed me again." Calypso finished her coffee and stared towards the beauty of the sea.

"You can understand why the Russians want Turkey can't you? That's the shortcut to the world for their ships and they don't control it." Constantine mirrored her gaze towards the shimmering blue.

Chapter 14.

He lay on the soft forgiving bed and looked at her. She was dressing for battle. A single birth and alcohol abuse hadn't ruined her body. She leant in towards the mirror. He looked at how her waist still tapered in before flaring out to form an exquisite arse, barely covered in the palest of purple tiny lace knickers that hid nothing. Her matching bra presented her breasts in the mirror as she applied barely visible eye makeup. Her skin a perfect shade of honey, her hair falling down like the finest waterfall, tangled by a naughty breeze. Every man would look at her tonight when she entered the room. Joel could not take his eyes off her.

"What are you looking at? Have you got a hard on?" She giggled.

"No, it's just that my underpants are too small."

"Come on pretty boy, get dressed we have to be there in an hour. Dont forget the syringes. I've got mine in my hair. Are you nervous?"

"Of course."

It wasn't far from the Bosphorus Hotel to the Embassy but Calypso couldn't 'teeter' any distance in her high heels, they were simply a statement to complement her legs. They took the five minute journey in silence, just holding hands on the tired 'springy' back seat. They were the 'perfect' young couple. She was sober, he was drug free, they were both beautiful. They walked from the taxi towards the elegant wide steps of the Embassy building. Inside could be seen black and white clad waiters with trays of champagne flutes.

"Are you going to drink?" Joel quietly asked.

"No, I daren't, can you get me orange juice?" She squoze his hand and glanced at him.

"Course."

They were 'unfashionably' early; there were about ten people in the room. Constantine spotted them, left the small group of men he was talking to and came over.

"You scrub up well." Calypso smiled as he approached wearing the compulsory black tie and dinner jacket.
"It's a facade, I have a Stanley knife in my pocket."
"Does the Ambassador know?" She asked.
"No, he thinks I'm just a big boy."
"And are you?"
"Ask Joel." He replied, glancing at him.

Calypso turned towards Joel.   *Privy Councillor?*

"Is that the Ambassador, over there?" Joel asked
"Yes, the Right Honourable Sir David Allenby. Do you want an introduction?"
"No, not really, Why are diplomats always stick thin?"
"You will notice that most diplomats are thin and most people in the Consular Service or the military are not. It's simply a class control thing. Diplomats are control freaks including their own bodies whereas Consular chaps are a bit more easy going."

Connie suddenly took a short sharp breath and stiffened up as a group of four men entered the doors. A large sand coloured dog with salivating jaws was ordered down in the halled entrance. The waiters with silver trays looked nervously at it as it slobbered all over it's arse before resting it's huge head on it's front paws. It's eyes looking upwards at the influx of smart people.

"Which one is it?" Joel asked.
"The tall one with the moustache."
"Do you think he'll recognise you?"
"Not sure. Maybe not. I don't intend to chat to him anyway."

Joel glanced at Calypso, she was staring at Sosa and he was staring at her.

"Well. That didn't take long did it?" Joel commented.
"He is rather handsome." Said Calypso.
"In a deadly sort of way." Muttered Constantine.
"I take it he can speak English?" She asked.
"No idea, it's not a requirement for torture. Screaming's the same in any language."

A circulating waiter passed close by, Constantine swapped his empty flute for a full one.

"I take it this is the first time you've seen Sosa since your 'event'?" Joel asked.

He could see Constantine almost shaking, his thin frame stiff within his immaculate clothes, his skin white and taute, his forehead and upper lip damp with nervousness. Calypso hadn't noticed, she was trying not to glance over at Sosa but failing.

"Yes, the first time. How are we going to do this?" Constantine asked.
"Just watch." Calypso said.

Calypso left them and started to move. She was a big female cat, a lioness prostrating herself onto the African dust, wagging her long fascinating tail around before a young virile strong lion.

"Hello." She paused "You noticed me then?"
"How could I not? The most shimmering brightest light in the room."

She held out her hand vulnerably drooped and deceptively limp. He took it, stooped to kiss it but then retracted.

"And you are?" She purred, lowering her eyelids.
"Balian Sosa. Major Balian Sosa."
"Major. Are you a soldier? You look like a soldier, tall, handsome with a dashing moustache. Tell me how many times a day do you shave?"

Sosa laughed.

"I'm not a regular soldier, I work for the Turkish Government, intelligence, that sort of thing, and it's twice."
"What about other bodily requirements?" She stared directly into his dark brown almost black eyes.
"At least twice a day, sometimes more, it depends on the woman."
"I'm a very capable woman." Their eyes refused to disengage. Glued by powerful animal attraction.
"I can see that. Could you cope with a twice a day man?"
"More if possible."

Sosa laughed as he threw back the champagne and called the waiter for another.

"You?" He asked.

"No, orange juice, alcohol makes me frisky but dries me out if you know what I mean."

"No, you'll have to explain that to me later." He touched her arm as he said the word 'later'. The other three men in his group imperceptibly moved away sensing the moment.

"Now, why are you here? What do you do?" What's your name?"

Calypso backed off slightly moving him further away from his group. She took a sip of her orange juice.

"My name is Calypso Fortnum-Guinness." She used her maiden name, it always sounded so much more impressive than Calypso Clay. "I'm just a recovering alcoholic who came along for a ride to escape rehab."

Sosa was surprised with her truthfulness.

"Is that sensible?" He asked.

"No, probably not, but then again do I look like a 'sensible' woman?"

"Definitely not. You look like a young prancing filly that can't keep still and is ready to race."

"You've been to Cheltenham then?"

"Every year, never miss." The statement fitted his voice, public school with no hint of an accent.

"I have to go back to my group, they'll think me rude, how long are you staying?" Calypso asked, moving closer to him so that their arms touched.

"About an hour, I have to circulate, you know, talk to some people."

"Nodd to me when you're ready to leave, you can walk me back to my hotel." She looked at him and paused. "That is if you want to."

Sosa looked at her.

"I want to, there's just one thing."

"What is your 'one thing' Major Balian Sosa?"

"I have a dog."

"I'm not fucking your dog."

Sosa was knocked back by her bluntness but quickly recovered.

"No! No! No! But he'll have to be in the room with us or he'll scratch the door down and bark forever."

"Is that it in the hall?"

"Yes."

"What's it's name?"

"Boga, it means 'Bull'. "

"But he's not a 'Bulldog'?"

Sosa smiled.

"No, but he is my dog, he's my shadow."

In a second she was gone, heading across the room towards Connie, Joel 'et al'. She knew he was looking at her arse as it joined in with the rhythms of her high heels.

"Things OK?" Constantine asked.

"Yes." She smiled. "He's going to walk me back to my hotel in about an hour."

"OK Joel and I will leave in about half an hour, we'll be in Joel's room next door, when you're ready just bang on the wall or the door, anything." It was as though all the blood had gone from Constantines face, replaced by liquid fear, ice cold hate and green dripping revenge.

"Introduce me to some other people then. I can hardly stand here on my own when you two disappear."

"Yes! Yes! Of course. Come over here with me."

"Miles, Miles, I'd like to introduce you to two friends and associates of mine, Mr. Joel and Ms Calypso, they're helping me on a project."

Joel and Calypso shook hands with a tall thin strong American man with a long powerful face and light brown, almost blonde hair that still retained the thickness of youth.

"Joel, Calypso, this is Miles Copeland, he's head of the CIA station in Beirut. God knows what he's doing here, maybe you can weedle it out of him." Connie laughed nervously.

"And what are you doing here Mr. Copeland?" The directness of Calypso's questions were always deflected by the sheer power of her presence and beauty. Miles Copeland swept back the thick hair that was about to fall over his face.

"Please call me Miles, I'm escaping my noisy three sons who are totally obsessed with Rock Music for some ancient quiet culture." He lied.

"He's trying to sort out the Philby mess." Constantine whispered in her ear.

"And where's Mrs. Copeland? Does she like Rock music?"

"In Beirut and no she doesn't, she's more of a Doris Day girl."

"I'm not."

"I can see that, let me guess." He paused to look over his champagne flute at her. "I would say Bob Marley."

Calypso was annoyed at his astute inference but he was right she loved Reggae music.

"Are you always so perceptive Mr. Copeland?"

"It's the job I do." Calypso turned towards Constantine but both he and Joel had gone.

Major Sosa caught her eye and nodded.

"Please excuse me Miles, Geoffrey, but I have to go." There was a glancing pause.

"It's a 'woman' thing." She smiled. "Lovely to meet you both." She handed her half empty glass of orange juice to Miles Copeland, turned and left. She knew they would be discussing her arse as she made for the wide doors. Balian and Boga were waiting in the hall on the other side of the doors.

"Madame. Would you like an escort to your hotel?" He purposely sounded French, emphasising the second syllable of 'Madame'.
"Do you have a big cock?"

Balian Sosa recoiled at her words before replying.

"Yes"
"Then yes please."

He proffered a fake bow as he moved beside her and with her as they descended the wide marble steps. Her stilettos trip, trip, tripping as they descended. Boga was slobbering obediently on his left.

"Shall we walk or ride?" Their eyes were riveted together at every opportunity.
"I'd like a ride please."

Sosa nodded to a footman doubling as a parking attendant for a cab. The footman waved and within two minutes a Mercedes drew up.

The reception staff immediately stiffened the moment Sosa walked into the hotel, almost to attention. More of fear than respect. The middle aged concierge bowed to Calypso as he handed her the keys. It was a convenient bow as he didn't have to look into her face or for that matter Major Sosa.

"Your keys Ma'am, Good evening." It was only just evening, six fifteen, the sun was beginning to weaken and slip away, going somewhere to rest and become strong ready for the next day, the next dawn. Calypso took them without response. Sosa noticed the room was on the second floor.

"Lift or stairs?" He asked. Calypso glanced down at her shoes.
"Lift it is then." The three of them entered the small wood panelled lift. Boga didn't like it and slobbered over the floor. Calypso and Sosa were silent. He slipped

his right hand into her dress and felt her breast, gently kneading her nipple and cupping her into his hand relishing the weight and feeling of her femininity. The wooden cage juddered to a halt and the doors cranked open. Calypso's breathing became faster and noisier, half sexual excitement half absolute terror of what she was about to do. What she had to do. 'What if the dog went mad when she did it?'

"Does the dog have to come in?" Calypso asked as she shoved the key into the round door knob.
"He'll only whine and scratch if he doesn't, Don't worry he won't tell anyone." Sosa laughed.

Calypso kicked off her shoes as she sat on the bed. Balian Sosa took off his jacket and carefully placed it over the back of a chair. He pointed to the corner of the room and Boga slunk into it, resting his huge head on his huge paws. He stood in front of her quivering as she stroked his trousers. Teasing with her tongue on the fabric, finally she unzipped him and undid him, letting his trousers fall to the floor, stroking it before reaching inside to get it out.

"Oh God, it is one." She whispered to herself as she ran her hands all over him.
"One what?" Sosa asked as he eased her bra below her breasts.
"One of those that curve upwards and so big."
"Turkish Delight - full of Eastern promise." He laughed as he pushed into her receptive mouth. Her right hand held him, whilst her left hand gently squoze and fondled his balls, they were a lot bigger than Boga's.
"I was rather hoping for something white and wet, is there a lot in here?"
"Yes." Sosa was succumbing to the delicious sensations sweeping through him.
"I want to do it standing up against the wall. Take your shirt off." she commanded. He drew away to take it off. Calypso stood up and slipped out of her dress. Sosa was looking at her, almost panting with excitement, she'd gone to the reception with no knickers on. Calypso took hold of his cock and led him across the room to the side wall. He was very wet, so was she. He nearly lifted her off her feet as he pushed into her, the curve and hardness moving deep inside making her moan with new sensations. Calypso could see Boga looking at them with uninterested eyes. He'd seen it many times before she thought. God she'd never felt like this, his rhythm was getting faster, more urgent, his hands were all over her, wanting to invade every part of her, the curve of his cock sent her into delirium with every thrust. His breathing was rapid, hers was rapid, he closed his eyes as muscles pumped exquisite relief into her. He hardly noticed the needle going into his right shoulder. Calypso pressed the red jewel down, nothing happened for eternal seconds then eyes opened as realisation flooded into them. He dropped to the floor.

Calypso frantically banged on the wall with the back of her clenched fist, it didn't sound very loud, had they heard? She grabbed his discarded shoe and banged on the lilac wall. Sosa was crumpled on the floor but his eyes were everywhere, darting, left, right then at her. She couldn't look. The dog hadn't moved. Her room door was locked, she'd have to let them in. She felt entirely inappropriate in a peach satin suspender belt pale stockings and her breasts platformed up and out by her pulled down bra. Now they were banging frantically at the door. Quickly she threw her dress over her body and let them in. Boga stood up, the line on his back starting to rise, his lips drawing back as a deep dark growl started. Calypso turned towards the huge Kuchi dog hissed and glared, the dog slunk back down to the floor.

"We have to be quick according to Sandra Lincomycin only lasts about five minutes."

Constantine was staring directly into the eyes of Sosa, standing there motionless except for a slight tremble.

"Come on Connie! Snap out of it! Help me get him onto the bed."

Connie broke away.

"I'll take his shoulders, you take his legs, after three!"

Calypso stood motionless by the foot of the large bed, The ecstasy of the last ten minutes now running down her left thigh. Then he was on the bed and within seconds Joel had found the vein in his limp left arm. Sosa's eyes started to flicker and dance in all directions as the Ketamine did it's work. Now, Constantine Ellis was ruthlessly calm as he took an orange stanley knife out of his pocket and pushed out the blade. He looked at it for a while. Sosa's eyes settled on it in wild futile fear.

"I'm going to watch your heart stop." Constantine Ellis was now an unstoppable animal. He had the blank deadly eyes of a tiger that was in for the kill. Sosa's eyes were frantically calling for help, the rest of him was motionless on the luxurious bed.

"I'm going! I can't watch." Calypso gasped softly.

"No! I need you for the dog, then you can go." It was a command started centuries ago and only finished then. Joel reached out and held her arm. Constantine's knife bit deep into the 'Turks' chest until it felt the hardness of bone then moved slowly but surely across his chest, down his chest then again down the other side. It was clinical, as though scoring the skin of a pig before the oven. Blood was flowing freely, hot red and sticky over the knife, over his hand, over his arm and now soaking into the bed. Three sides of an almost perfect square. Boga didn't like it growling into his front paws but not moving. Constantine lay the knife down on the bed and dug four fingers of each hand into the top cut till his fingers also felt bone. Looking straight into Sosa's eyes he slowly clamped his hands. With the strength of a driven man he began to pull the skin back. Calypso and Joel looked away. It sounded like wet velcro, blood was everywhere, the effort required lifted the body of the terrified Sosa. Joel wondered how a man with skinny arms and small muscles could bring about such strength. Sosa's eyes rolled up, voluntarily, involuntarily, Joel had no idea. There it was. Just like a medical mannequin, pumping violently, almost vibrating. He smiled as he picked up the knife again and moved down, lifting up his now flacid penis he sliced into the base, as it fell to one side revealing his scrotum the blood started to pump out in strong pulses as it emptied Sosa's body. Constantine Ellis didn't care about the blood, just guessing where the scrotum joined his body he cut away until it came away, joined by only a thin ribbon of bloodied skin he displayed it in front of Sosa's eyes. The eyes were now quivering as though in the last frantic movements of life. Constantine grabbed Sosa's head by his hair and turned it to look at the dog before throwing the bloodied meat in front of the still growling huge dog. Connie nodded to Calypso who after a second glanced at Boga. Within two gulps it had gone. The dog licking the wet, still warm blood from the floor.

"Inject the dog. " Constantine directed Joel.
"Help me Calypso."
Calypso Clay moved over, crouched down and cradled the huge head in her left hand whilst stroking the becalmed animal with her left. It was if the animal didn't feel the needle enter the folds of it's neck skin then after a few seconds it rolled over.

"Come here Joel, hold his head to one side I want him to see."
"I'm not sure if he can see Connie, I think he's had it."
"Just hold his head for me Joel. Please?"

Joel moved to the head of the bed and gently held Sosa's head on it's side.

"Calypso, you can go now."

Calypso quickly made for the door her olive skin now pale and different.

Connie moved over and looked directly at Sosa's eyes as he sliced down from under the right ear deep into it's throat. Pumping blood was instant, death was a minute away, heralded by eyes that clouded over with transparent pain. Moving back he stared at Sosa's heart. It was still. Sosa was reunited with his dog Boga.

"What are we going to do about all this?" Joel surveyed the two dead bodies and escaped blood.
"Nothing, put the two notices on the door 'Do not disturb' and 'Do not clean' go next door and get cleaned up. Calypso will leave with me, an hour later you check

out. Just you, not Calypso then come to the embassy, I've arranged a room for you, try and look as respectable as you can, it helps."

"What about the fact that there's two dead bodies here?"

"Eventually they'll go in, call the police, the police will realise who he is and call in MIT. They won't want to publicly acknowledge that one of their top intelligence officers has been murdered so they'll just be a very short public notification that Sosa unfortunately died of a sudden heart attack, everybody will assume that he died 'on the job' so to speak, no investigation, just a clean up."

"Remind me to never cross you Connie." Joel said as Constantine Ellis and Calypso left the room.

"You can never cross me Joel. I love you." Connie remarked in a throw away comment as he closed the door.

Chapter 15.

The long, long white roof of the big Citroen estate was easy to spot in the almost empty car park of Bristol Airport.

"Hello you three, all relaxed and refreshed after your 'Business Class' exotic trip." Jonathan beamed as he got out to open the tailgate.

"Just killing time, you know how it is." Calypso spoke in a sombre voice. Jonathan picked up on the collective mood. The car rose slowly as the engine powered up.

"So, anybody going to fill me in on your plans?" He asked.

"Bicknor, tests, food, rest then maybe a walk." Joel muttered.

"All of you?"

"Probably." Confirmed Constantine.

The journey continued in silence. Crossing the cattle grid brought about the usual involuntary intake of breath as the tight confines of the lane suddenly opened up to the lush green open gently descending pastures.

"Any new people since we left Mr. Jonathan?" Calypso asked.

"No, that is unless you count a new nun in the kitchen."

"Is she beautiful?" Constantine asked.

"You mean is she a good capable cook?"

"No. I mean is she hopelessly naive, young and very beautiful?"

"Yes she is. Her name's 'Sister Claire'." Jonathan brought the big silent car to a halt in front of the big glazed doors.

"My office please for tests." After a few minutes Trevor bustled in, a softly expanding man with a round affable face who always did as directed, did it well and never did anything wrong.

"Well! Well! Well! The travellers have returned. Say AAAAH!" Trevor wiggled the swab around Joel's cheeks and tongue.

Joel put her bag on the chair in front of her dressing table. Calypso lay back on her familiar comfortable bed.

"Suppose you're going to run off with Constantine now I've done my bit?"

"No."

"Come and lie next to me, I need time to get over what's just happened. I can't believe we just walked away from that horror and nothings going to happen."

"Believe it, that's how government agencies work, they're all powerful. They don't have rules." Joel stroked the tangle of her hair as she snuggled into his body.

"Are you really going to help me kill Hetty Betts?"

"I said I would. You need to give me some information, a way in."

"Well I can give you the name and address of her 'Womens Refuge' she mainly takes in drug addicted prostitutes who's pimps keep them on a leash with a mixture of romantic promises, violence and heroin. Then of course there's CND but she's well protected there."

"Sounds like she's doing a bit of good to me."

Calypso turned her head from staring at the ceiling to look at him. Joel was still staring at the ceiling.

"In any other circumstances I'd agree but unfortunately she undoubtedly caused the death of my husband and deprived my son of his father and that most probably caused the suicide of Jonny Conrad who was the best lover, my first lover, I ever had."

"Better than me?"

There was a pause.

"Yes but he was the first and I was very young."

"Better than Major Sosa?"

"That was different, you can hardly compare luring somebody to their death with sex to the first flush of youth."

"Yes but was it good? Was it exciting? Did you enjoy it?"

"Yes, his was longer than yours but not as thick, you couldn't tell after Constantine cut it off but it was one of those Eastern things that curved upwards. I had him fuck me up against the wall so I could feel it. I don't want to talk about it anymore. Go outside."

"What?"

"Go outside, then come back in as the Sultan of the Topkapi Palace, I'm just your concubine, your sex slave, you don't care about my feelings at all, you just point at me and I know what I have to do. Don't speak."

Joel went out of the room, fortunately there was no one on the landing, no one around. He waited two or three minutes then brusquely opened the door strode in and noisily closed it. Calypso was sat by the pillows of her bed wearing a white soft dressing gown. He pointed with one finger at her, she moved slowly, moving two pillows to the foot of the bed placing one on top of the other, sitting on them she undid his belt, his top button and slowly unzipped him putting it straight into her mouth as she moved his trousers and underwear down to the floor. She made him very wet before releasing him and lying back on her bed, her dressing gown wide open, her breasts aching for his touch, her lower back now high on the pillows, her legs as wide apart as she could manage, her eyes closed as ------------------.

"I'm going for a walk with Connie this afternoon." Joel was lying beside her as she shook and moaned slightly as she finished off the Sultan's pleasure with her own hand.

"I'm going to spend the afternoon in a hot bath, try and soak away those memories. Now we're here it's as though it was some awful dream, a nightmare. God, I could never do what Connie did to that man."

"That man wasn't very nice to Connie in the past, bit like you and Betts."

"Yes but us women are much kinder killers."

"See you at dinner." Joel rolled over, kissed her on the forehead and searched for his underpants.

It was a biting easterly wind, sub zero temperatures all of the grey day. The last thrust of winter before the closing sun had it's way and gently coaxed the buds from the trees, the flowers from their buds.

"Let's go down to the church on the river bank, we haven't done that walk for some time." Constantine said as he wrapped his muted red tartan scarf around his neck tucking into his Barbour.

"OK, any reason?"

"No, I'd just like to think a bit."

The drive was nothing in a car but it took at least ten minutes walking then the sharp rough track downwards to the left then the green meadow banks of the river, dark, cold and irresistible.

"It's going to be cold in the church." Joel said as they entered the lych gate.

"That's OK." It was as though Constantine's heart was already cold.

Joel and Constantine sat together on an oak pew looking at the altar.

"Did the Ambassador know what we were up to?"

"Good lord no, I told you, you, and of course the medics who stitched me up are the only ones who know the truth."

"Won't they put two and two together about Sosa?"

"Why would they, could have been anybody, the Russians, the Armenians, maybe the Americans, nobody knows what really goes on and who's really who in that game. It's all smoke and mirrors."

"You mean in your game."

"Yes, but I suspect it's your game too, my handsome prince." Connie reached out for Joels hand and smiled.

"What are you going to do now Connie?"

"Go back home to mothers in Oxford, stay there for a while till she totally annoys me then slip back into work I suppose."

"Anywhere in particular?"

"Beirut, easy access to Syria plus they've got really good French restaurants there."

"What will you be?"

"An archeologist of course doing research into ancient Hittites sights."

"What really?"

"Trying to find out if the station there deliberately let Philby flee to Russia."

"You will be careful won't you?"

"Why? I'm a useless fucking eunuch."

"Because your mother would be upset--------------------and so would I. How are we going to stay in touch?"

"Do you want to stay in touch?" Constantine asked, turning towards Joel in the pew.

"Very much so. You?"

"Me too. Come on I'm really getting cold now. Just let me say a quick prayer. kneel with me."

The two young men both knelt together in the cold stone deserted church. Constantine whispered a prayer. Joel listened.

The walk back up the steep track warmed them up, their breath hanging and visible in the weak grey light of midday.

"Connie?"

"What?"

"Before we split up can I have a drive of your Bristol?"

"No, it's too complicated for you, it has a 'freewheel'."

Joel took his arm as he struggled up the hill.

"So where are we at the moment?" Edenson asked.

"I've been clean for six weeks, thanks for asking."

Daryl Edenson raised his eyebrows and rolled up his eyes in feigned exasperation. The journey up from London had been tedious; a large queue at the Severn bridge had delayed them for over an hour, fortunately he was using his boss's car and driver so at least it was reasonably comfortable in the back of the Rover.

"Glad to hear you're fit for work, your time here will finish at the end of this month, that's just ten days away so we need to know how you are going to achieve our requirement." Edenson chose his words carefully. Joel thought his face looked even fatter and whiter.

"I've told you, I want a fifty acre smallholding somewhere in Shropshire, Clun, Bishops Castle, somewhere like that will do."

Eden's exasperation became more pronounced.

"Here's how it works Mr. Joel, you do the job, successfully that is, then you may get your wish."

"Mr. Edenson, I need somewhere safe to live to stop me failing, my intention is to get married to a vet called Sandra and settle down. Now, as a compromise how about you locate a suitable property, rent it out for a year with an option to buy, that way we're both happy." Edenson didn't answer.

"What about Ms Calypso?"

"She's my way into Betts so I need to keep her happy if you understand? She has information and a way into a Women's Refuge that Betts owns and operates, it was funded by her late husband. Calypso blames Betts for his death and wants revenge. Calypso was instrumental in the resolution of Constantine Ellis's problem so she now thinks that I owe her one, which I do of course but she's totally unaware that we have the same goal."

"And what about your boyfriend Ellis? I believe he's MI6."

Joel looked disparagingly at Edenson.

"He's not my boyfriend. He is a very good and close friend."

"MI6 are all Oxbridge, Eton or Harrow, most of them are queer, if they weren't when they started they usually are when they've finished."

"What about CND? Has your lot got anyone inside that group?" Joel asked.

"No, they're all Duffle coats and dog collars, it's not a good fit for ex police or military, that's why we're spending a lot of money and time talking to you. I suggest you get religion pretty quickly, or at least buy a coat. Is the umbrella still OK, you haven't fired or damaged it have you?"

"No it's OK."

Chapter 16.

"Sandra, it's me."

"One moment, whilst I sit down again, my wellingtons have crumpled and are failing to support me. Are you ill, dying, or just want something?"

"Just wondered if you're free this weekend?"

"A herd of Herefords to vaccinate, a flock of chickens with red mites, and some horses to look at, other than that I'm totally free. Why what's in that devious head of yours?"

"Wanted to whisk you away for a surprise weekend that's all."

"What, in that baby's rattle of a mini?"

"Well we could use your Volvo if you want."

"I would want, yes, I can hardly get into that thing. Where we going anyway?"

"Can't say or it wouldn't be a surprise would it?"

"Are you clean now?"

"Yes of course, have been for over a month now. Pick you up on Friday morning."

"It's a long weekend then?"

"Longish, bring a few pairs of pants and socks."

"Anything else, you know, condoms or anything?"

"You know I hate them, you'll just have to get pregnant."

"Aren't people supposed to get married before that stage?"

"Yes. See you Friday morning after you've done your cows and chickens."

"Joel?"

"What?"

"Dad's not well, I'd like you to meet him this time, not hide or run away."

Joel's heavy breath was audible down the phone.

"If that's what you want Sandra that's OK. Have you ever introduced a man, a boyfriend to your folks before?"

"Never had a boyfriend before."

"So he's going to assume it's an important step for you, his beloved daughter."

"Probably."

"And is it?"

"Yes."

"See you on Friday."

"Can't wait, drive carefully in that box of yours."

Mr. Jonathan's ears were finely tuned to the cream coloured phone at the other end of his office.

"Just a reminder Mr. Joel, you've only got ten more days with us."

Joel looked at the deceptively 'comfortable' Jonathan sitting behind his desk, the seemingly chaotic paperwork cluttered on it just a smokescreen for all enveloping observations and incisive perceptions.

"Working on it Mr. Jonathan, working on it."

"Good."

"I'm away this weekend and leaving here at the end of the month." Joel took her hand as they walked down towards the river pastures. Calypso was strong now. Somehow the Istanbul interlude had given her strength, made her realise that rules don't matter, only yourself and the people you love matter.

"What am I going to do without you?"

"You'll never be without me but I think, if we're honest we know that eventually our lives will take us in different directions."

"I'm going to make a large-ish donation to Betts's Women's Refuge Charity and arrange a visit to hand over the cheque, I want you to match it then I'll have an excuse to bring you with me. Apparently they don't normally let men into the place but I'll insist."

"How much?"

"Two thousand pounds."

"Wow! That is large-ish."

"Can you match it?" Calypso asked as they moved from the rutted stone lane onto the struggling green grass.

"I think so, I'll have to talk to someone. What's it called?"

"The Island Sanctuary."

"In Manchester I presume?"

"Somewhere yes, the address is a secret."

"Shall we walk round to the village and get a pie from the Post Office."

"Love to." Calypso tucked herself into and onto his arm. There was no else in sight, high above them two Peregrine falcons slowly circled, their deadly eye searching for tiny movement. Their lunch.

"Apparently they're the fastest bird in the world."

"How fast?" She asked.

"Over two hundred miles an hour in a steep dive, in fact they're the fastest animal in the world."

"Amazing!" Calypso stopped and stared up at the two birds.

"After all this is over what are your plans?" Joel asked.

"Go to Martinique, find my real father. If he's alive, You?"

"Marry Sandra, live on a small holding in the Shropshire hills, have a few kids, if we don't have kids have some sheep."

"Do you love her?"

"I suppose I do, not like Janey, not like you but she saved my life and I sort of owe her."

"Is that good enough reason to marry and spend the rest of your life with her?"

"Yes; but there's more she's just so, so."

"So what?"

"So dependable, practical, sensible."

"Sexy?" Calypso looked out from under her hair.

"Yes in a needy sort of way. I've got to be there for her, make her happy."

"Lucky girl. Chicken and mushroom or steak and kidney?"

"Chicken and mushroom for a change."

They leant on the usual stones of the bridge parapet not looking at the cars and traffic that passed underneath.

"Two thousand pounds is a lot of money Mr. Joel." There was a telephone pause. "Isn't there another way? A cheaper way?"

"Not that I know of. You?"

"OK, go to the Lloyds Bank in the town in four days time, there'll be a cheque book waiting for you. Don't abuse it, and Mr. Joel-."

"What?"

"We expect value for money."

Joel put the phone down.

"You get all that Mr. Jonathan?" Joel quipped as he left the large office.

ntrance to Arrowsmith Farm came up quicker than he expected, the brakes caused his coat to fly off the front passenger seat and the ɔ 'chirp' on the dry tarmac. He hoped there was no one behind; he] his mirror.

"Hello you. You're early."

"You know me Sandra, couldn't wait any longer to be with you." He kissed her on her left cheek.

"You're so full of shit! - But I like it. Come on in, the kettles on."

Sandra made them two cups of tea in OXO mugs.

"So what's this surprise?"

"It requires a map, a blue Volvo estate and a long journey, so pack your bags and let's go, no knickers required."

"Is that a request or a demand?" She looked at him through a semi ginger frizz that had drooped over the side of her face.

"A request, I could never demand anything from you Sandra, I don't think I would ever have to."

Sandra and Joel looked into each other's eyes. God she was a beautiful person, there wasn't a glimmer of malice, an ounce of nastiness in her whole countenance.

"Which way?" She asked as they bumped up the track.

"West, go West?"

"How far?"

"About six hours west?"

"Think we'll be in the Atlantic Ocean by then, it's a Volvo not a boat."

"Just turn left and head for Birmingham."

opened 1972

"Now where Mr. Navigator?" Sandra asked as they approached Spaghetti Junction.

"Follow the signs for Ludlow."

"There aren't any."

"How about Worcester?"

"Think we've just passed it."

"Kidderminster?"

"Maybe."

"Lunch?"

"Definitely, but not on a motorway, I want a nice country pub."

Sandra had cod and chips with mushy peas, Joel had sausages and onions with mash and gravy. The pub didn't look nice, just a large red brick square but the food was good.

"We need some petrol, who's paying?" Sandra asked as the thirsty Volvo headed towards Ludlow.

"I am of course, can't invite a beautiful woman away on a romantic weekend and expect her to pay for the petrol can I?"

"Since when have you been so courteous?"

"Since I fell in love."

"Who with, your exotic rich helicopter girl?"

"No with a vet farm girl."

"Really?" Sandra glanced at him as she was driving.

"Really. Now keep your eyes on the road."

Sandra changed gear then put her hand on his leg, squeezing his knee.

"Turn left here, head for a place called Lientwardine then turn right for a place called Clungunford."

"Are you sure we're not in Wales?"

"I'm sure."

"Those names don't sound very English."

"Well they are."

The scenery started to change, large blank hills started to appear to their right stone walls started to appear instead of hedges. Somehow the grass seemed tougher.

"Here! Here! Turn right here and go slowly."

The dirty blue car trundled along at a sedate twenty miles per hour.

"How much longer have I got to keep this up for?" Sandra asked.

"About two seconds, we're here."

A weathered leaning 'For Sale' sign towered above a small wooden plaque hanging on an almost broken wooden farm gate.

"Bird on a Rock. this is it." Joel jumped out and opened the gate. Up the track could be seen a grey stone plain house and some outbuildings, It started to rain as they pulled up in front of the dark red wooden door sheltering under a porch.

"What is this place?" Sandra asked as she got out stretching her body.

"It's our home."

"What on earth are you talking about?" She looked at him as he stood behind the open car door staring at the no-nonsense house.

"It's our home if you want it to be. Forty eight acres of small holding nestling at the foot of the Long Mynd hills, what more can a girl want?"

Sandra looked at him before the tears came.

"I can't, Dad's got cancer and Mum would never leave Arrowsmith, it's their life."

"This could be our life Sandra. I can wait for you, I can wait as long as it takes."

She closed the car door and walked round to him to take his arm.

"Lets go look inside."

Inside were yellows, blues, browns and creams. Black and white cracked uneven tiles on the ground floor, plain wood floorboard upstairs. Remnants of life made it untidy, bit's of ripped lino, old fly blown lampshades, white sinks that weren't white, a bath with added green, faded thin curtains hiding dead flies and cupboards hiding the detritus of farm life.

"I love it, how can you affo-------."

Joel cut her off.

"I've got one little job to do then it's ours but we can move in when we like. At the moment I've rented it for a year, just in case you didn't like it." He lied.

Sandra walked around the empty cold house touching the painted walls.

"I love Rayburns, this one's old but I bet it still works, they go on forever, too heavy to move."

The views from the small upstairs windows just rolled away with green fields, she held two fingers of his hand.

"What about children?"
"I told you, I hate condoms so as many as come along."
"We need to get married first, that's what normally happens."

She turned to look at him, the floorboards creaked as they moved towards each other.

"Whatever you say," Joel whispered before kissing her gently. "Shall we go and buy a bed?"
"Where from?"
"Shrewsbury, There's one of those new shops there, you buy it in bits, bring it home and screw it together, bit like Meccano. We can put it on your roof rack."

"Let's walk around the fields first." Sandra kissed him again.

The intermittent cold sparse rain went unnoticed.

"Needs a lot of work, gates to be fixed, hedgerows need re laying, some of the stone walls are down in places."

"We've got plenty of time, a lifetime." Joel said, glancing at her round red face with wet hair.

"Better go and buy a bed then before the shops shut. How long does it take to get to Shrewsbury from here?"

"About half an hour, we need to get a few essentials as I'm homeless in ten days' time."

"And you intend to move in here?"

"Well I've got nowhere else, except that is, a very damp and falling apart yurt in Wales and I don't fancy that, bad memories and a big mistake led me to you know where, you know what, then you saved my life."

The half grass, half cobbled yard in front of the house was a perfect place for a long tender kiss. The yard sloped gently away from the house and barns down to the short drive that led to the road. It was a peaceful panorama.

"When we get home tomorrow I want you to come in to meet mom and dad." Sandra said as they made for the door.

"Do you like the colour of the door?" Joel asked.

"I love it, I love everything about the place. I love you." It was the first time she'd said it. "Strip the doors, stairs, landing and bannister rails back to old pine, new curtains and lampshades and that's it, I don't want to change anything else, just clean it up. Let's see if we can get the Rayburn going tonight." She grabbed his arm as they headed through the door.

"Cancer of what?" Joel asked as the Volvo bumped it's way slowly down the drive to Arrowsmith.

"Cancer of the pancreas, it's horrible, mom isn't coping very well with it, the MacMillan nurses come in every other day to bath him. He's on a morphine drip so the end can't be far away."

"And you? How are you coping?"

"I'm using work as an excuse, fortunately there's plenty of it, I'm always busy. Here we are. Oh God, mom's outside, she's started smoking again, dad doesn't know, well she thinks he doesn't, he's no fool, he'll smell it on her, he won't say anything though. It's too late, everythings too late." Tears welled up in her eyes as she stopped and put the handbrake on.

"Are you close?"

"Very, dad was the one I went to as a little girl when I was upset or wanted something. He'd always give me what I wanted, mom wouldn't, she was far more strict, I know this sounds silly but it was almost like a female thing, fighting for his affection. I always won, He was always telling me I was the most beautiful girl in the world. I'm very obviously not."

"I'm not so sure about that. I'm with your dad." Sandra smiled and patted his hand. "Come on, let's go in."

Christopher Hardwick looked him up and down from his entangled bed.

"What's a handsome young bloke like you doing with my daughter?"

There was no introduction, no time for niceties or smiles. He wanted to know.

"I was a drug addict, I overdosed, Sandra saved my life. Like you, I think she's the most beautiful girl in the world." It was a brutal answer to his violently direct question.

He stared at him again before his strained face collapsed into a broad smile as he proffered his only hand that wasn't connected to something.

"You hurt her Mr. ----------?"
"Joel, my name's Joel."
"You hurt my precious girl Mr. Joel and I promise you I'll haunt you forever." He laughed, allowing saliva to dribble out of the left side of his mouth. Sandra quickly wiped it away. "Now tell me all about yourself and what you hope to do. Your first born will be a girl, call her Grace after my mother." Sandra prodded him in mock embarrassment.
"Sit, sit down on my bed."

It was very late on Sunday evening when the little green mini trundled slowly over the cattle grid and onto the immaculate drive of Bicknor. Joel had been thinking the whole journey, the mechanics of driving a welcome backdrop to his thoughts. Connie was set to leave on Wednesday, he had to leave on Friday. Calypso was staying on for a while. After her apparent surge of strength she'd disclosed to him that she was finding it difficult to get over the sights and sounds of Sosa's death. Joel was beginning to worry that she might be having second thoughts about Betts.

"Hello you, Thought you'd be asleep." Joel had seen the light on under her door, tapped and entered. She was sitting at her dressing table in a pink dressing gown just staring into the table mirror.

As she got up the soft gown fell open. She took his hand and led him to bed.

"It's been an empty weekend without you. I've just been rattling around here, lost with nothing to do."

Joel lay beside her. Things had changed, Sandra wasn't in the same league as Calypso yet she now held him. He was obligated. He felt guilty. Christopher Hardwick somehow had commanded him to cherish his beloved girl. Now he was playing a part, using Calypso, pretending to help her when in fact Calypso was his route to a normal life. A life he now wanted more than ever.

"Where are we with Betts?"

"Have you got the money?" She asked looking up at the ceiling as she moved the dressing gown away from her body, laying it out before him, inviting him in.

"Yes, I've got to collect a cheque book from the bank tomorrow."

"OK, I've spoken to her on the phone, she's over the moon with the money, even so It was difficult to get you in. They don't like men. I told her you were a recovering heroin addict with a personal fortune and were almost certainly gay."

"Thanks!" Do I have to walk in a mincing way and wave my hands about a lot?"

"No, but you do have to prove to me right now that you're not gay."

Joel couldn't resist the effect she had on him and she knew it.

"Just do it, don't consider me just do it. I like it like that, you know I do."

It didn't take long.

"When are we going?" Joel broke the silence after he'd rolled off her.

"Thursday."

"Have you got an address?"

"No. We have to wait at the front entrance to Manchester United football stadium."

"I hate football." Joel laughed.

"Let me check." Her hand grabbed his scrotum. "These two are nearly the size of footballs."

"Don't kick them whatever you do." Calypso gave him a little squeeze before letting him go and laughing.

Constantine Ellis was already sitting at their breakfast table when Joel entered the dining room, it was surprisingly full and busy.

"Hi." Joel said as he pulled out a chair and sat down.

"Hello. How did your weekend go?"

"Life changing."

"Really?"

"Really. Think I proposed to Sandra."

"Sandra, not Calypso?"

"Sandra, she's good with sheep."

"Is that a requirement for marriage?"

"Definitely."

"What about us?" Constantine asked.

Joel looked directly into his eyes.

"Us-------------- friends forever."

"Only friends?"

"Dear friends. ----------- What are your plans Connie?"

"Well, mothers allowing me to build a small cottage, a bungalow I suppose, in the grounds of her house and I intend to set up a very exclusive printing press, you know individual copies of the classics for collectors, that sort of thing. Of course I'll be doing quite a lot of research about the books in the Middle East."

"No real change then."

"No, we can never really escape can we?"

"No but I'm going to really try."

"Why?"

"Because I dont really like who I am and what I do. I want a normal boring life."

"They won't let you. You know that. What are you having?"

"Just grapefruit, toast and marmalade."

"Where's Calypso?"

"Sleeping, she had a hard night last night."

There was a knowing glance.

"Wish I had?" Connie laughed.

Chapter 17.

"What's this?" Joel asked.

"Manchester United scarfs, we can hardly hang around the front entrance without one can we?"

"Where on earth did you get these from?"

"Manchester. There's these new inventions, a telephone and the Post, you're such a luddite."

"No I'm not, I've got an electric razor." Calypso stroked his chin.

"If you have you haven't used it today."

"Designer stubble today."

"More like laziness, have you cleaned your teeth?"

"Yes."

"Washed behind your ears?"

"Yes."

"Behind your foreskin?"

"Yes."

"Come on I want to check. You're to stand to attention, naked in front of me. I'll pull it right back and look."

"And then what?"

"If it's clean I'll suck it." She smiled and softly giggled.

"What if it's not clean?"

"I'll smack your bottom and then suck it."

Calypso led Joel up the stairs.

It was a grey drizzle of a morning.

"Four o'clock tomorrow afternoon is the rendezvous, we'll go in 'our' Mini to Ledbury Station, get a train to Birmingham then change for Manchester."

"And why is 'our' Mini going to Ledbury and not Hereford or Gloucester?"

"The parking's free."

"Oh!" Joel responded wondering how on earth she knew that but didn't want to ask.

"Constantine leaves on Friday."

"Does that sadden you?" Calypso asked.

"Of course, I'll miss him. He's taught me a lot."

"What, like how to murder someone in the most ghastly way."

"No, he's taught me that Latin and the Classics matter even in today's modern world."

"Rubbish they're just a secret handshake for the elite rulers."

"I take it you don't like him then?"

"I love you and you love him -------------- as well as Sandra."

"You're all different. I love Connie's mind, his knowledge, his sophistication, I love Sandra's grounded, down to earth easy complete love."

"And me, what about me?"

"I love your beauty, your kindness, your flaws and your body. I've got a hard on now just saying that."

Calypso lowered her eyelids and grinned as she put her hand under the table.

"So you have, can't waste that, come on Sultan, upstairs. I want to be your concubine for one last time." Calypso led the way out of the dining room.

"I presume you'll be spending the night with Connie." She paused on the stairs.

"We're going out for a meal."

"And I'm not invited?" She paused on the stairs and looked at him.

"No."

Joel loved going in the Bristol. It just smelt so opulent, the ride seemed sure footed but still comfortable. Constantine was so confident driving it, changing gear without the clutch, using the free wheel. It was an 'old money' car.

"I've booked a table at the Green Dragon in town, from what I hear the food is pretty good."

Joel felt underdressed, he hadn't got any 'evening-ish' clothes, never mind the 'dickie bow' that Constantine was wearing with such easy panache.

The dining room was understated and under full, just three couples all elderly. They took a corner table near the window. Constantine took charge of everything and ordered champagne for them.

"You will come and visit me in Oxford won't you?" Connie asked looking over his flute of champagne.

"Yes of course but I've got a few things to sort out first?"

"Edenson?"

"Yes."

"How are you going to escape from him Joel?"

"Not sure, maybe I won't, maybe I'll just get too old and they'll get someone else."

"Maybe?-----What are you eating?"

Joel picked up the dark green leather menu.

"Well considering where we are it has to be a choice between wild Wye salmon or prime Hereford beefsteak." Joel pondered. "I'm going for the salmon, asparagus, and new Pembrokeshire potatoes."

"I'm with you." Concurred Constantine. "Always."

The two young men looked at each other.

"Seriously, if you're ever in trouble or need any help, come to me first ----- please." Connie said.

Joel reached out to touch and hold for a moment Constantines hand.

"Thank you." A woman with permed grey hair and red spectacles two tables away glanced over to them. She didn't smile.

"What are you going to do about Calypso? You know she's in love with you."

"We've spoken about it, I've told her I'm going to marry Sandra, anyway she's going off to Martinique in search of her father, her real father."

"Will you sleep with me tonight?" Just sleep, I want to wake up in someone's arms. I've never done that."

"Not even when you were a boy with your Mom?"

"Especially with my Mom. I had a nanny, she was nice but 'employed' if you know what I mean."

"No I don't but I can guess and yes I will."

This time Constantine reached out with his hand. The woman glanced again and whispered to her correspondingly grey husband.

Calypso was right, the parking was free at Ledbury, a railway station that time was forgetting. Everywhere she went she attracted stares and attention, it was as though she was one of nature's stars so brilliant you could not but look. They walked over the bridge and stood together on the functional platform waiting for the blunt ugly diesel to appear from the deceptive dip and throb it's way towards them. There were eight people waiting to get on. When they had, the doors closed and the engine roared.

"I've never been to Manchester." Joel said as the blunt nosed powerful unit curved towards the platform towing it's reluctant carriages. "Look at that."

"Look at what?" Calypso asked.

"Look at the name of the engine 'Long Mynd'."

"What's it mean?"

"It's a range of hills directly behind the smallholding Sandra and I are going to live in after this --------------------- ." Joel stopped himself saying 'this job'.

"After what?" Calypso asked.

"After this 'holiday' at Bicknor." He replied.

"You have got it bad haven't you?"

"I just want a normal life, I had one once before in Wales but she died in an accident and things went bad from thereon in."

"And you can't have a normal life with me?"

"No. You're not normal Calypso, you're the most beautiful sexy woman I've ever met but I don't see you shopping in Tesco's or unblocking a toilet."

"Neither do I, come on pretty boy let me sit by the window. I want to watch the rain as we get near Manchester. That's all it's famous for you know, rain and football. Don't leave your bloody umbrella on the train whatever you do."

"What's the plan when we get there? Will it be Betts that meets us?"

"I doubt it, I've no idea who will meet us, we just stand there in our scarfs till somebody says hello."

"Are you still comfortable with this?"

"Yes."

It started to rain as the train belched out a last cacophony of noise and blackness to drag itself into the station.

"What time is it? We've been standing here for ages." Joel moaned.

"It's ten past five, the rendezvous wasn 't till five'o'clock, we were early."

A drab woman in a gabardine mack and a shopping bag walked up to them. She looked the type to wear a plastic rain hood but she wasn't. She wore a deep purple beret with a small brooch and feather on the side.

"Follow me." She said.

"Excuse me?" Calypso responded.

"Follow me if you want to go to 'The Island', to be honest I'm not very comfortable with him. We don't allow men in." Her voice matched her mack, dull, grey, hard and resilient, there for the long haul. She headed towards a dark blue Austin eleven hundred. A small woman was sitting behind the steering wheel.

"Is that Betts?" Joel whispered to calypso.

"No." The gabardine mack woman overheard.

"Ms Betts sends her sincere apologies she can't meet you today she's in bed with the flu. I'm the manager. My name is Ms Williams, I'm authorised to process any business you wish to conduct, show you around and allow you to talk to any of the current occupants who wish to talk to you."

Joel looked at Calypso as they climbed into the back of the car. He carefully placed the umbrella on the rear parcel shelf.

"Shan't be needing that now. The rains stopped." He said to Calypso.

Joel wondered how he was going to explain to Edenson how he'd spent two thousand pounds for nothing. Calypso had deflated.

The streets of Manchester were continuously busy, red brick to grey to red brick to steel to red brick to glass as houses jostled with small factories, homes with businesses. Then, without noticing it changed to better bigger houses, substantial red brick with sandstone windows and doors. Detached, set back and protected by trees and established vegetation Joel noticed a road sign 'Sale' the driver said nothing, gabardine mack said nothing. The journey lasted about fifteen minutes then the car slowed and turned into the small front driveway of a large detached house with dirty windows, a semi derelict VW Camper van tucked under a tree and an old boat on an old trailer almost blocking the other side of the house. The curtains looked dirty and lifeless as though they were tired of hanging about. There was no number or house name. Everybody got out. Joel left the umbrella in the car.

Once inside, gabardine mack softened.

"Well, this is it, 'The Island Sanctuary for women.' The only one in Manchester, probably the only one in the North of England. I'm Rosie Williams, the manager. This is Hilda, our driver and fixer of everything. Please sit down."

Calypso and Joel sat down together on a long red dralon sofa. The curtains to the large bay front window were almost drawn , the ceiling light needed to be on.

"Now, what can I get you to drink?"

"Tea will be fine ----------------- for both of us." Calypso responded glancing at Joel.

Rebecca hesitated as she came into the room with the tea tray. The sight of a man was unusual in the house, in fact she hadn't seen one before. She placed the tray on the small table in front of the sofa.

"Hello, why don't you get another cup and sit down with us for a moment?" Calypso's face had changed into an oasis of sympathy, Joel had never seen that look before, it was as though there was a sharing of some unstated suffering. Rebecca glanced at Rosie Williams who was standing by the door for tacit permission. Rosie just nodded.

Rebecca returned after a few seconds with another cup and saucer.

"My name's Calypso, I'm a recovering alcoholic and this is Joel he's a recovering heroin addict."

The brutal immediate disclosure jumped several stages of introduction and opened a door. Rebecca relaxed into the corresponding dralon armchair.

"I'm a friend of Ms Betts, we're here to help with a donation." Calypso half lied.

She was a thin girl, barely a woman, maybe nineteen or twenty wearing tight black trousers, a blue blouse with a thick dark blue cardigan over the top. Her face was somehow damaged as though smiling was difficult, her hazel eyes cautious and nervous. Joel noticed there were small round marks on her bare feet.

"It's cold, you should wear socks." Joel said looking at her.

Rebecca immediately tucked away her feet, embarrassed he had noticed the burns.

Calypso poured out the tea.

"Do you feel OK telling us something about yourself?" Calypso asked.

Rebecca's eyes dashed between the two of them.

There was a long silence

"I've only been here for three weeks, Mom got a new boyfriend, he liked a lot of sex, first with her and then with me."

"How old are you Rebecca?" Joel asked.

"Seventeen, her boyfriend, Aldane was his real name but mom called him 'Danny', was very big if you know what I mean and really hurt me. He quite liked hurting me and mom was out of it most of the time on amphets or gear, whatever Danny gave her. He used to keep me locked up in my room, then when he felt like it he'd do it to me with mum watching, he liked that, then he'd grab her by the hair and make her lick and suck him. He got a real kick out of it, sick bastard. If I said anything or didn't do as he wanted, he'd burn me with cigarette ends. I put up with it for ages 'cause of mum, she was just a wreck. He didn't care about her at all. Eventually I couldn't take it anymore, scared stiff he'd make me pregnant so I climbed out of the window and ran away. Nowhere to go, no money, lived rough on the streets, police picked me up for begging, they didn't know what to do with me so i ended up here."

Calypso got up and hugged her as Rebecca burst into hopeless teenage tears.

"Any biscuits?" Joel asked, to break the moment.

"No, we don't have biscuits here." She sobbed, holding her head in her hands.

Rosie Williams came back into the room.

"Can you go and take the washing out of the machine and put it in the dryer Rebecca, make sure that nothing woolen goes in the dryer won't you?"

"Yes Ms Williams." Rebecca left.

"You're doing marvellous work here Ms. Williams, we're so glad to be able to help." Calypso said.

"Rosie, please call me Rosie. Ms Betts is the real force behind it, she's the real inspiration behind it all she had a major donor that kept us going but unfortunately that person died, I've no idea who he was, she never said, so things have been difficult since. Four thousand pounds is an awful lot of money and is greatly appreciated, it will keep us going for over a year."

"How many women have you got here?" Joel asked.

"Ten at the moment, we can take twelve, there's another girl due in today, not sure if she'll make it or not, it's always a bit uncertain."

"Is this the only house the charity has?"

"Yes and we don't own this, it was bought by the donor I mentioned, he actually owned it, we just have free use of it, apparently when he died it reverted to some huge trust he had somewhere in Ireland."

"The Fortnum-Guinness Foundation." Calypso added.

Ms Williams looked astonished.

"You know it?"

"Yes I know it." Calypso glanced at Joel as she handed over the two cheques with Joel's cheque on top. "We need to be going soon, train to catch and all that, thank you------------------------."

There was a slamming of a car door outside then loud raised shouting voices.

"Why do I have to come to this fucking place? What the fuck is it? Where the fuck is it?"

Dusk was beginning to draw in, a white ageing Morris Isis had pulled up on the gravel outside the front steps. The driver, a middle aged woman was trying to calm down a young dirty unkempt looking woman in her early twenties.

"It was here or prison Angela, you know that."

"No it fucking wasn't I haven't done anything wrong. They can't touch me. I'm gone, goodbye."

"Angela, this is your bail address, if you're not here then we'll have to report that and then you'll get picked up, then it is prison which is a lot more uncomfortable than here. And yes eating pre packed sandwiches in Sainsbury's is most definitely wrong especially if you have no money. Just think a little bit before you go storming off."

"I was fucking hungry! Fucking starving! I'm fucking pregnant or hadn't you noticed and I've just hitched all the way from Cardiff, took me three days and four fucking blow jobs to get away from that Welsh cunt."

"That's why you're here love, come on in, let's get you some food, a nice hot bath and some clean clothes. Come on love, we're here to help you."

Susan Sanderson led Angela Whitworth gently by the hand up the three sandstone steps to the front door.

Angela Whitworth was very obviously half-caste, just like Calypso. There was an immediate bond that happened in the flicker of an eye. The same flicker caught sight of Joel.

Angela baulked at the last step.

"I thought you said there was no fucking men allowed at this place. That was obviously a fucking lie."

"There isn't, he's just a businessman with some money for us. Come on now, let's get you settled in. Calypso moved out of the front door and held out her hand towards her. As she moved closer she could see white stains down her cheap black skirt and an obvious smell of stale sex, smelling like fish. The two women helped the distraught defensive girl into the big house,

Joel stood to one side of the wide steps as the trio of women moved into the house. He'd lost Calypso, she was now totally involved in the fate of the girl.

"We'll catch a later train." She whispered to Joel as they passed by. Angela by now was beginning to collapse into intermittent sobs and sniffles before being sat down at the small table. Calypso, Rosie Williams and Susan Anderson shared her suffering as they touched, stroked and comforted. Mugs of tea and some sandwiches were brought in by the driver of the eleven hundred.

"Thank you Hilda." Rosie said. Hilda disappeared as discreetly and quietly as she had appeared. Like Joel, barely noticeable, just part of the scene.

"I couldn't stand it anymore, it wasn't so much the pain it was the uncertainty. You know, one minute he's telling me how much he loves me, can't live without me, buying me small things, making me a cup of coffee, all normal like. The next day he'd beat the shit out of me, kick me out to do tricks, scream at me not to come back unless I had money for him, it was like living with a nutter, which one was him. Trouble was I did love him, he's the father of this child for God's sake."
"You were picked up hitchhiking in the middle of a main road Angela, that's not a normal thing to do is it?" Rosie quietly said.
"I know! I know! But I ain't normal am I? And what did the fucking police do? Nothing! They took me in, kept me for a few hours whilst they thought about things then just kicked me out. Didn't even give me a cup of tea or a sandwich, that's why I had to hit Sainsbury's. I was starving and then there's my baby, If I'm starving it he will be as well."
"How do you know it's a boy Angela?"
"Dunno, I just do." Calypso put her hand out on top of Angela's.
"I knew my baby was going to be a boy as well. You just somehow know." Calypso said.
"Come on, let's get you a hot bath, some clean clothes, a good meal then bed, we can do the paperwork tomorrow."

Rosie Williams led her away to safety, Angela wasn't a pretty girl, mousy straight dirty hair, messy zits on her nose and face where she'd been picking and scratching, beaten brown eyes that sat close to a big wide nose. Her skin was coffee brown. There was no mistaking her African genes.

Calypso moved back towards Joel. Ms Williams appeared after a few minutes.

"Thank you so much for your support, it means so much to us." She shook their hands. The gabardine mack had just been a defense for a warm gentle caring person. "I'll get Hilda to run you to the station, the trains run every hour to Birmingham, please give me a call if you want to come again." Rosie Williams handed over a plain white card with a number on it to Calypso and Joel. "Oh Ms. Betts apologises again for not being able to meet you but she asks if you could join her on the Aldermaston March at Easter, she says if you could come on the last leg, that's Easter Monday she will be leading the March on that day, it will finish about three in the afternoon then you'll be able to have a good catch-up, she's really looking forward to seeing you again Ms Calypso."

A subdued Calypso took the card and put it in her handbag.

"Yes we'd love to, please tell her we'll be there." Calypso glanced at Joel.

It was dark by now. The big house front porch was lit by one feeble bulb in a white glass shade that was covered in dead flies and spiders webs. It made the porch entrance look soft and welcoming.

"I think I own this place." Calypso said to Joel as they clambered into the back of the Morris.

The cold wet green Mini started at first push of the big button. The train journey had been almost in silence, the rattling and swaying allowing their thoughts to wander and settle.

There was no moon, the hill up to Bicknor seemed narrower and steeper, a female deer and her tiny calf looked into their lights before melting into the dark wet woods.

"Joel?"
"What?"
"I don't want to kill Hetty Betts."

There was a huge silence in the noisy Mini.

"OK.----------------- Any reason for the change of heart?"
"Maybe I got things wrong. Maybe it was the 'Guy' chap in St Petersburg who persuaded him to defect. I just don't know. Maybe Jolyon was right supporting her. After all, it was probably his decision if he was doing anything wrong with his plane and what Betts is doing now, somehow seems right. Maybe She wasn't totally responsible for his death. I just don't know anymore."
"OK, why don't you sleep on it?"
"I will. By myself if you don't mind."

"Course not, do you want to go on this march?" Joel asked quietly, frantically looking for options.

"Yes, it'll look bad if we don't."

Joel let Calypso out at the front door then parked around the back. He picked up the umbrella and thought about Edenson. He'd be on the phone first thing tomorrow.

"Do you mind Mr. Jonathan, this is a business call from Mr. Edenson. It's a bit sensitive."

He did mind but Joel was leaving in three days time so reluctantly he left the room heading for the kitchen.

"I don't see anything in the papers. You know, 'Prominent CND leader dies of a sudden heart attack' that sort of thing. I'm a little disappointed to say the least."

"She's changed her mind."

"Who?"

"Calypso Clay, nee Fortnum Guinness, she's my way into Betts, her wish, her intention was to kill Betts, she blamed her for the death of her husband Jolyon Clay and her lover Jonny Conrad but you know all this of course. Anyway, yesterday we went to this women's refuge as planned to hand over the cheques and carry out the action. Betts was ill in bed with the flu so it was a disaster in every way. Calypso was so taken in and impressed by the place that she's changed her mind."

"So we're two thousand pounds down and nothing to show for it."

"Well you could say it's gone to a very good cause, they do seem to be doing a lot of good there."

"We're not interested in doing good Mr. Joel." Edenson snapped. "We're interested in saving the country from the Russians. It's a bit more important than saving fallen women."

"There is a possible option." Joel said.

"What?"

"We've been invited to head the Aldermaston Peace March with Betts on Easter Monday, just the last day"

There was a long silence.

"But to be honest Mr. Edenson, I don't really want to do it."

"What you want is of no consequence Mr. Joel, we can soon inform Her Majesty's Prison Service that we've managed to detain the escaped person wanted for the murder of Leonard Flower Welham, plus we then won't have to be buying a piece of Shropshire. The choice is yours Mr. Joel. We require a result this Easter Monday." The line clicked off.

"You off then?" Joel walked into Connie's room without knocking. Constantine Ellis was packing to leave. Three identical brown leather suitcases were on his bed. The clothes in them were folded neatly. His Loackes and Church's shoes in individual paper bags.

"Yes this is it, the end of our beautiful romance." Connie said without looking up.

"Rubbish, you know that's not true. I'll need a Best Man when I marry Sandra, I'll need a Godfather for our kids. I'll always need you in my life." There was a silence across the bed. "To teach me about Latin and the ruins of Palmyra.----------No repercussions from Turkey then?" Joel asked.

"No. I told you there wouldn't be. It's finished now. Mother's allowing me to build a bungalow come printing press in the grounds at Oxford and the office wants me to start in Beirut in the New Year. You can visit me there if you like?"

Joel didn't answer and picked up two of his Smythson cases.

"Put those down Joel."

Connie moved close and kissed him on both cheeks.

"Thank you, thank you for your support, your understanding, your friendship." Constance Ellis looked directly into the face of Joel before clasping him in his arms.

"Ok! Let's go, grab the cases."

Joel picked up the cases and followed him down and out to the dark green Bristol. Within moments it cruised quietly away up the long drive til it disappeared into the trees.

The place seemed different without him. No point of reference. At lunch there were just the two of them.

"It's no fun having you all to myself." Calypso could see and sense Joel's incompleteness. "And next week I won't even have you."

"What are you eating?" Joel asked.
"Ham salad."
"Can you get me the same?"

Her immediate reaction was to say 'get it yourself' but instead she got u went to the hatch.

"Make that two, Chef please."

"Thanks. We never had sex, despite what you think." Joel looked over the stiff white table cloth at her.

"It's none of my business what you two got up to."
"Of course it is." Joel retorted. "We were lovers I don't want you to think you were part of a threesome."
"Were Joel? Were? What's changed?"
"Everything, since Manchester the fun has gone, you've changed."

Calypso took a sip of water.
"Life just got serious again Joel, maybe I have a reason to get up in the morning, a reason to not go out and buy a bottle."

"That's good then. Isn't it?" He looked at her lovely eyes."
"Very good." She said.

'Two ham salads' a voice rang out.

"I'll get them, do you want salad cream?" Joel asked.
"No, Mayonnaise please."

"How long are you going to stay here?"
"Not sure, I'll stay til after the march, see how that goes then make a decision."
"Mmmmm, sensible." Said Joel reaching for a bread roll and a scroll of butter. "It's only three weeks away. The evenings are getting a lot lighter now, have you noticed?"
"Not really but I suppose you're right. How about an early dinner, say six-ish then an evening walk?" Calypso asked.
"That sounds nice, according to the weather the showers are clearing from the west, should be a nice pleasant evening."

Calypso smiled and reached out to touch his hand. Now it wasn't sexual, just friendly. Joel stood up and left the dunning room. He couldn't remember what she was wearing.

"Special place one or special place two?" Calypso asked as Joel closed the solid back door.

"You choose." He said.

"Special place one. I can kneel and say a little prayer in front of the crumbling Virgin Mary."

"What you going to pray for?" Joel walked close by his side as she took his arm.

"You and me of course."

"Thats nice."

They walked around the small church, down the rocky track, up the secret pathway between the brambles, along the top of the bank then down to the carved out alcove. Joel sat on the old stone bench as Calypso sank to her knees, clasped her hands and spent time silently talking to a painted concrete statue.

After about five minutes she got up and sat beside him looking down the growing spring pastures dotted with sheep and beyond to the now calm river. Her hand rested on his.

"So where do we go from here? Are you relieved about Hetty Betts."

"Of course." Joel lied. He wondered if it made any difference lying in a religious place.

"I know where I'm going Calypso, how about you?"

"I think I'm going to Manchester."

"Only think?"

"No, I am going to Manchester. Meeting those girls changed me. It just made me think what a pointless life I've led up to now."

"I'm happy for you Calypso. Really happy for you."

Joel put his arms around her and hugged her.

"I can't come this weekend Joel, Dad's taken a turn for the worst, it could be days, could be weeks, no one knows."

"Oh OK, I'm leaving Bicknor tomorrow I'll make a start cleaning and decorating and stuff."

"No. No. Please don't ,I want us to do it, you know, decide what to chuck what to keep, what colours go where, lampshades, curtains and stuff, just sort of camp out there till things are sorted here."

"OK will do."

"Joel?"

"What?"

"How would you feel about bringing mother to live with us?" She's not going to cope with dad gone and me gone. I want her to sell the farm and move in with us."

There was no hesitation.

"That's fine, it will be good to have some experience around us."

"Thank you. I was really worried about asking you. You are a love. C dash now, got some sheep to inject. Love you"

The word took him back to Istanbul, Ketamine and Sosa then by association Betts and his current predicament.

Joel knocked and walked into Mr. Jonathan's office with his room keys.

"Time to go Mr. Jonathan." It was a blustery on off sort of day, lots of clouds, some rain and a little sun.

"Well Mr. Joel you came to us with a habit, you leave with a green Mini, a rich girlfriend and best of all no habit. All I can say is well done."

"She's not my 'girlfriend' Mr. Jonathan, just a good friend and I didn't do it on my own, couldn't have done it all without this place. Thank you."

"It's just a business Joel, glad we could be of some help. Now what's next?"

"Well, as you know I'm moving to Shropshire to a rented small holding with Sandra, eventually we'll get married. I'll be back here in a couple of weeks to pick up Calypso, we're going on a 'March'."

"What do you mean 'a March'?"

"The Aldermaston Peace March, Campaign for Nuclear Disarmament."

"I never had you down as a peace activist Mr. Joel."

"Died in the wool hippy me! My mother lived in a yurt in wettest Wales, I had the most 'organic' childhood you can imagine."

"Doesn't say anything about that in your notes."

"No it wouldn't would it? It wouldn't say a lot of things like I was forced to kill a man I later found out was my half brother, forced to kill a very good man who just happened to make his money from illegal drugs but was doing a lot of good in the world, There's lots you don't know Mr. Jonathan."

"I think ---- Mr. Joel, it's better I don't know. I'll stick to managing this place."

The two men shook hands.

Out in the back square there were a few cars but no dark green Bristol. Calypso carried one of his bags. The boot of the Mini could only take one bag so the other three were packed onto the back seat. Joel unclipped one of the rear windows and shoved it open. If it rained on the way the Mini tended to steam up unless there was a draught flowing through.

144

"Well this is it, see you in two weeks, I'll be here on the Saturday night so we can get away very early on Sunday morning."

"Will you sleep with me that Saturday night?" Calypso asked.

"Do you want me to?"

"Very much so. I feel we've drifted apart and I don't like it."

Calypso put her arms around his neck and gave him the longest tenderest kiss she could.

" Wow! Where did that come from?" Joel said.

"From the bottom of my heart, a special place I'll keep just for you."

"See you in a couple of weeks."

Joel eased himself onto the small seat, pulled out the choke half way and pressed the big button on the floor. He slid back the driver's window.

"Don't forget to press the button in as you apply the hand brake." She smiled as she touched her lips and then his lips through the open window.

He wanted to look back as he drove off but stopped himself before wiping his eyes.

'Bird on a Rock' farmhouse looked solid cold and grey as he pulled up in the rough yard. He sat in the car listening to it tick and click away as things cooled down. The front door was a deep red colour, he'd wash down the front porch tomorrow and clean out the porch light. He liked the colour of the door and thought that Sandra liked it too. Sandra had managed to get the Rayburn going last time so it can't be all that difficult. As far as he could remember there were some logs in a box at the side. The umbrella was on the small back shelf of the Mini. He had no idea what he was going to do about Betts. Calypso wasn't in the game anymore, neither was he really, once again he was being forced into doing something he definitely didn't want to do.

Chapter 18.

It took three days to get the phone 'on' but by Thursday 'Clungunford 573' was connected to the cream coloured dial phone that sat on an old shelf just before the front door. On the shelf were two old directories, a 'Yellow Pages', a local code book cluttered with biro'd numbers and some years old copies of 'Farmers Weekly'. All of them were faded and dusty. Between the shelf and the door were some old black iron coat hooks. Joel hooked the umbrella on one of them. The phone was dirty with flie 'blow' and dusty with dust. He'd clean it tomorrow or maybe try to replace with a new one but for now he'd ring Sandra.

"Hello, it's me ringing from 'Clungunford 573', your new home."

Joel's cheeriness was soon dispelled by the sobs and sniffles on the other end.

"He's gone, Dad died this morning." Sandra's distressed voice was not a good start to the re reconnected phone.
"Oh, I'm so sorry."
"Well don't be. If he'd been a horse I'd have put him down weeks ago. It was horrible Joel. He knew what was happening despite the drugs, his eyes were frightened, I could tell he was really scared, he was 'compos mentis' right til his last breath, then he just stopped breathing as though the money had ran out on a phone."
"I've never asked but did he know it was terminal?"
"Of course pancreatic cancer is hardly a common cold just hope it's not hereditary, I really wouldn't like to go like that."

"How's your mother taking it?"

"It hasn't really hit home yet, she's been too busy making arrangements and things plus there's the farm to run, the stock still has to be looked after and fed."

"How about you?"

"Oh you know me, fat, frizzy and capable, I'll get through it."

"Do you want me to come down?"

"No, you'd only be another worry for mother. Let me get this sorted and the funeral over then I'll bring mum up for a couple of weeks break that'll hopefully extend into forever."

"What about all your animals? Sorry I shouldn't be asking these sorts of questions at this time."

"Yes you should, it stops me collapsing into a sobbing little girl who's just lost her dad, the dad who was always there for her, the dad who told her she was the most beautiful precious girl in the world."

"Well he was right. You are."

Sandra's sobs flooded the phone.

Time passed quickly at 'Bird on a Rock' farm. Joel decided he'd have to swop the Mini for something more 'practical' after the 'March'. 'The March' was a source of worry, he was looking forward to seeing Calypso again but dreading an 'opportunity' that would set them apart forever. 'Maybe that was a good thing', he thought to himself as he hosed down the aged concrete floor of one of the small barns. 'Sandra would see her as a threat if they ever met'. 'Yes, the thing he had to do would finish his relationship with Calypso and that was good!' It was cold in the barn, Joel headed inside for a cup of tea. The large enamel kettle was perched on the plate attached to the flue pipe, it kept it just hot, all he had to do was put it on the hob for a few seconds and it was boiling. The Rayburn was a godsend, he kept it going all the time, their Scandinavian 'kit' bed was in the kitchen, it was the only room in the house that was warm. If Sandra's mother came to live with them he'd have to think about some form of heating upstairs.

"Do you have to go on this 'March' thing? I want to bring mother down at Easter." Sandra spoke softly down the phone as though her mother was listening.

"Yes, I have to go, it's sort of a 'work' thing, to do with that chap Edenson, I don't want to do it but I have to, you know money and that sort of stuff. Plus I promised Calypso, she's involved with one of the founders of CND, a woman called Hetty Betts so we've been invited to head the march. A lot of people are expected to turn up from all over the world, even some survivors from Hiroshima, it's a big event."

"So what are you? Some sort of part time government spy?"

"Something like that. Is the farm up for sale yet?"

"Yes, the man planted the sign at the end of the drive two days ago, everytime we go past it mother bursts into tears as though someone's selling her life or rather their life. It's horrible, the sooner we're away from here the better.

"What about the stock, all the animals?"

"There's an auction next month."

"Can't we use some of them here."

"No, Shropshire's more sheep than cattle. We'll buy some from local markets.

"I've been cleaning out the barns today, cold work but I enjoy it. It gives me a sense of satisfaction, haven't had that since my farming days in Wales."

"I want us to be together Joel, miss you, have done since Kathmandu."

"Just get this job over then come up. I miss you too."

Joel flung one bag onto the back seat of the Mini. He'd have to stop in Craven Arms and get petrol. It was only a couple of hours to Bicknor, He'd suggest a walk down to the Post Office for a hot pie lunch. The thought of seeing and being with Calypso excited him, he wasn't comfortable with it, he'd rather be washing down the front porch or cleaning windows or sweeping the yard. The umbrella was lying on the back parcel shelf. Was it Calypso that excited him or fear, nerves, anxiety, call it what you will of what he was about to do, had to do, so that his normal life with Sandra could continue. Yes it was the fear, not just Calypso he decided.

It cost three and six now to fill up the Mini. It was always going up, never down.

"Hello you." He said climbing out of the car. Calypso had been waiting in the dining room, looking out the front windows to spot the little green car coming down the long drive. It took her back to Lugalla, looking out of the window and watching Jonny's blue Porsche driving away from her. She'd moved from the dining room to the front of the house as he pulled up.

Putting her arms around his neck she kissed him on the lips.

"Am I allowed to do that now you're a respectable Shropshire farmer with a farmer's wife."

"She hasn't moved in yet so yes."

"Wish I was Sandra?"

"Well you're not, plus you'd never make a farmer's wife in a million years."

"What would I make?"

"A women's rights crusader. Oh and the sexiest fuck I've ever had."

For a second Calypso became serious then laughed. Her 'beau jangle' hair moving with her smile, her serious thoughts melted away by his eyes.

"Let's walk down to the Post Office and get a pie, you can tell me all the gossip and plans for this weekend."

"Hang on there, I'll dash in and get my coat. Don't go away."

Mr. Jonathan's office window slid noisily open.

"Vehicles parked around the back please Mr. Joel."

"Oh good morning Mr. Jonathan, how are you? Very nice to see you again." Joel sarcastically responded.

Mr. Jonathan rolled up his eyes.then shut the window.

Bicknor was a safe place to be, the length of the drive compressed by comfortable conversation. The long descent into the village now negligible as arms entwined.

"They do 'pasties' now as well as pies."

"I find the thick crust a bit too dry to eat on pasties. I'm going for steak and kidney." Said Joel.

"I'm for a pastie, who's paying?"

"It's your turn, I paid last time." Said Joel.

"I haven't bought any money." Calypso giggled.

Joel looked at her.

"Why does that not surprise me? Tell me about this weekend. What's the plan?"

"Well we make our way back to Bicknor, go up to my room and you fuck me, then we have dinner then go to bed and you fuck me, then when we get up and you fuck me before breakfast. How does that sound?"

"And after?"

"Tomorrow morning we leave for Aldermaston and join the march. I've made a placard for us each, do you want to look?"

"Of course! Can't wait."

"Not such a nice day as yesterday is it?" Calypso stated as they walked out to the Mini.

"Those placards will never fit inside the car." Joel stated.

"Yes they will, put the card bit between our seats and the poles sticking out of the back windows."

"We'll get stopped by the Police."

"No we won't, anyway if we do I'll just smile and pull my jumper down."

"You're such a tart."

"I know but that's what does it for you isn't it Joel?"

"Yes." She put her hand on his trousers.

"Stop it. I'll get a wet stain." Calypso laughed.

"Which way?" Joel asked.

"No idea, women don't do maps."

"Those signs on the placards make me think of you with your legs wide open."

"Good! Actually It's taken from the position of two semaphore flags for the letters 'N' and 'D'."

"Is it really? Who told you that? "

"Hetty, Hetty Betts."

"Have you seen her then?"

"No but we've spoken on the phone quite a lot. Turn left here. There they are. There they are."

"How are we going to work this? What about the car?"

"Well we park the car up then join the front row of the march, we march for a few hours then you get a lift back to your car, drive it up to the front of the march and so on. According to Hetty there'll be minibuses and cars going back and forth all the time for people."

Calypso got out of the car and grabbed her placard. She seemed to forget all about Joel. He was now just the taxi driver. She was focussed on a woman he presumed to be Hetty Betts, Short, thin, nondescript looking with short curly mousy hair and glasses wearing fawn crimplene trousers, a blueish blouse and a light brown car coat. She was holding a pole at one end of a large banner that read

CND - Ban the Bomb.

A man with a grey beard was holding the other pole. Behind were the marchers, All shapes and sizes, all colours, groups, couples, foursomes and loners. Some singing, some playing guitars, some pushing prams, some leading dogs, some pushing pushchairs, young and old, five or six abreast as far as could be seen. Placards and banners were 'de rigueur' for the marchers. Joel parked the Mini up in a pub car park, grabbed the umbrella and rushed to join Calypso and the plain little woman.

"What have you brought that for?" Calypso almost hissed as it reminded her of her original intentions.

"It might rain." Joel whispered back. Calypso looked down her eyes at him.

"Hetty! So good to see you again after all this time." Calypso gushed. "You haven't changed a bit. You're looking well."

The two women embraced for a second, having to keep pace with the march.

"Well this is a bit different to getting whisked off in a plane to the South of France. Have you still got that little green sports car? I was so envious of that car. What with me, Veronica and Jonny all squashing into that 'bouncy' Mini of his. You looked so sophisticated in it."

150

"Yes I've still got it, had a bad crash in it a while back so it's been rebuilt but I still have it. It's part of my youth, part of my life, I intend to keep it till I'm old and grey." Calypso laughed. It was as though her old suspicions and dislikes had vanished. Now they were old friends with shared experiences. "Let me introduce you to Mr. Joel, he's the other half of the four thousand we gave to 'Island'."

Henrietta Millicent Betts stretched out her right hand in front of the walking Calypso and shook hands with Joel.

"I can't thank you enough Mr. Joel, keeping 'The Island' going has been a struggle since Jolyon passed away but your donation is a tremendous help to us."

"It's my pleasure Ms. Betts."

"Oh please call me Hetty, everybody does."

The front rows of the march was a 'who's who' of the CND movement, an Earl and his wife, senior members of the clergy, academics, scientists, actors and film stars led the procession of thousands, all seeking peace, no wars and definitely no terrible nuclear weapons. The march came to a crossroads, four Policemen in helmets, raincoats and large white gloves acted as traffic lights allowing the march to proceed through in alternating segments with the crossing traffic. 'They would be there for a long time'. Joel thought, The march was huge, groups from most cities and large towns in the UK and many groups from abroad. There were lots of beards, beads and sandals. The rain was intermittent, Joel used the umbrella to shelter Ms. Calypso and Ms Betts who, for most of the time were deep in conversation. Joel could sense that Betts was a little uncomfortable with him being excluded from their conversations. He was an important donor, she didn't want to lose him. She swapped places with Calypso.

"What's your connection with Ms Calypso Mr. Joel?" She asked as she slotted in beside him.

"We met in a rehab, I was recovering from heroin addiction, she was recovering from alcoholism."

There was a considered pause.

"Ah! That explains a lot. And were you both successful?"

"Yes, it was a very good rehab, very exclusive, very expensive but very good."

"You're a rich man then Mr. Joel?"

"No." But Ms, Calypso is."

"Men with no money don't hand over cheques for two thousand pounds to a Women's charity."

"Some do Hetty, Some do."

"I'd like to take you somewhere Mr. Joel?"

"What do you mean?"

"Well in about an hour we'll be passing an unmarked entrance to few of us, a secret few, we call ourselves 'Spies for Peace' will break awa the lane and demonstrate outside the security gates at the end of the lar it's to take some photographs of the place."

"What's an RSG?" Joel asked .

"Regional Seat of Government. A vast underground bunker for the government and it's cronies to shelter in and run the country whilst the rest of us die in our millions. There's a few of them dotted around the country but this is the main one. In spitting distance from London but far enough away to be safe from the bomb or maybe bombs."

Sandwiches were handed out as they walked, there was no stopping for lunch. Ham and tomato, tomato and cheese for Vegetarians or tomato and cucumber for Vegans. Drinks were water or water. The closer they got to London the more people joined.

"Isn't that a good thing that the government is at least thinking about what to do if there was a nuclear attack?"

"There is no defense to a nuclear attack Mr. Joel, it wipes out everything and carries on killing for decades after. RSG's will be under the control of the Military, not elected civil leaders. Britain would become a military dictatorship as well as hell on earth. That's why what we're doing is so important. It's life or death Mr. Joel. Here we are, come with me."

About twenty people from the front echelon of the marchers suddenly broke away at some unspoken, unseen signal and headed down the lane. Joel tagged behind Betts, Calypso stayed with the march. Joel was sweating with fear and anxiety. He liked Hetty Betts, and admired what she was doing. Envied her passion. It was clouding over. Maybe it was going to rain again.

The manicured lane dipped down into a hollow, stout galvanised steel posts carrying barbed wire and electric elements surrounded a large grass area. Behind it was just a steel door entrance to a large tunnel. Military Police manned the gates from a substantial 'blockhouse'. Alsatian dogs strained on long chain leashes as the group approached the gates. Hetty Betts was totally engrossed, chanting and shouting at the surprised police behind the wire, an officer was on the phone in the blockhouse, reinforcements would soon be arriving to disperse them, two or three members of the group started to openly take photos. It started to rain.

Besides her face and hands there was only one other place of bare flesh on Hetty Betts. Her crimplene stretch trousers were short. Her shoes were blue 'bumpers', thick rubber soles with a canvas top. She wore no socks so her lower calf and ankle were visible. The scene was getting more chaotic as people started running about waving their placards and shouting at the police. God! What was he

? The Women's Refuge was a good thing. She was right, Nuclear bombs were able bad things. The world would be a lot safer without them. Hadn't it been seconds away from armageddon over Cuba. The TV had been telling people to hide under the kitchen table. For Gods sake look at Hiroshima and Nagasaki, millions dead instantly. A kitchen table was just not going to do it. Then there was Sandra and her mom, 'Bird on a Rock' Farm. The future, his future, their future.

Joel moved in close to Hetty and clipped the umbrella to open. Holding the stem and turning the handle left made the small green button pop out. No time to think! No time to think! Just do it! It's him or you all over again Joel. Just do it, doesn't matter if it's a her. Doesn't matter who it is, we're all going to die someday anyway. Just do it. Joel held the umbrella a few inches away from her calf and pressed.

He didn't feel anything. Hetty didn't feel anything, well didn't seem to, she leaned down for a second and scratched at the little red mark. There was no blood. Joel held the umbrella over her. By now the rain was heavier, someone called a halt and the group moved back as they huddled together to check whether or not the photos had been taken, then they moved off back up the lane to rejoin the march. Joel collapsed the umbrella as the shower eased. Pressing the button he tried to press the button in and turn the handle back, to no avail, it wouldn't turn back and the button wouldn't stay in.

"Are you alright Mr. Joel? You look a little pasty."
"Yes, I'm OK, this is the first time I've been a demonstrator, it unnerved me a bit." He lied. She smiled and tugged his sleeve.
"Come on let's go find Ms. Calypso."

The group disappeared into the crowd, Hetty and Joel rejoined the front row. Hetty took the pole from Calypso.

"I was getting quite attached to that pole." Calypso said with a smile. Her smile instantly disappeared when she noticed a small green button sticking out from the handle of the umbrella. Joel was looking the other way marching along chatting to a man with a beard whilst holding the umbrella over Hetty and a bit of himself. 'He'd fired it off somewhere safe - that's it' thought Calypso, 'he was having to use it as an umbrella and had made it safe'. Her convenient logic brought back her smile. Anyway Hetty looked and seemed fine.

Dusk was approaching, the march was ending for the day as people drifted away.

"Tomorrows the big day." Hetty said, "You two going to be with me? We think there'll be more than ten thousand people gathering in and around Trafalgar Square. The biggest demonstration ever. They'll have to listen to us then." Hetty glowed.

"Well I am, Mr. Joel here has to get back to his wife, his mother-in-law and farm." Calypso wasn't pleased with Joel. She'd assumed he'd be with her and take her back to Bicknor. He'd only told her a couple of hours ago that he wasn't.

"Never mind Calypso, we have a hotel booked you can bunk in with me, we can chat about old times, tell me about your boy, does he look like Jolyon?"

Calypso smiled and nodded.

"I don't see as much of him as I would like, he's at Eton but yes he does look like Jolyon."

"OK, I have to go now, I'm so sorry Hetty but it's family stuff, you know how it is?" Joel chipped in.

"This is my family Mr. Joel, this and my refuge. Thank you again for your help and do stay in touch." Hetty Betts shook his hand. Joel looked at Calypso then gave her a polite public kiss on her cheek. She suspected something terrible. He knew, she could sense it.

"Give my regards to Sandra." Calypso politely said.

Joel nodded and left with his umbrella.

It took Joel four hours and two petrol fill ups to get to the gate of 'Bird on a Rock'. The house would be cold, the Rayburn would have gone out. It was just before midnight. Tomorrow Sandra and her mum would come and he'd be happy to see them. Anything but this awful numbness that surrounded him, his own thoughts that imprisoned him, walked with him wherever he was. He knew it would pass, it always did. Time would make it unreal. Distance helped. Sandra's mom had a dog, that would help, he wanted to get a sheepdog as well. He'd have to learn to whistle. He could whistle of course but not that loud shrill whistle generated by putting your fingers in your mouth, he couldn't do that. Miraculously the Rayburn still had a few red embers in it, he could get that going again with a few dry sticks then break the umbrella into pieces and burn it. Just in case Edenson had finished with him and wanted him out of the way. Anyway it would remind him, and he wanted to forget. There was no sleep that night.

It was six a.m. on Easter Monday morning. Hetty Betts rolled in pain from her bed onto the floor of her hotel room. In agony she crawled to the door of the adjoining bedroom where Calypso was. Feebly she knocked. Calypso opened the door.

"I need a doctor and an ambulance immediately." She screamed down the phone.

"Why Madam?" The Hotel receptionist was cool and calm as though it wasn't an emergency.

"Just do it. Ring '999' Room eighteen Ms. Hetty Betts she's been --" Calypso stopped herself. She's having a heart attack I think, I don't know, just get help quickly."

"Yes Madam."

Calypso went back to Hetty who was ashen grey, barely breathing, barely conscious. It took ages for the ambulance to get there. By the time they did Hetty Betts had stopped breathing.

Upstairs, on the floor of one of the small back bedrooms he'd found an old bakelite Pye valve radio. Joel had dusted it off and brought it into the kitchen. The fabric covered wire looked pretty ropey but he'd plugged it in anyway. The house still had old fashioned round pin plugs but nothing blew up or smelt of burning and after a while the radio warmed up and worked.

'And here is the news at eight a.m. on the morning of Monday the fifth of April. - Prominent CND founder and chief strategist Ms Henrietta Betts has been found dead in her hotel room during the annual Aldermaston Peace March. It is believed Ms. Betts suffered a heart attack. Police say that foul play is not suspected.-----------------------------.

Joel turned the radio off and moved the kettle onto the hob. The phone rang in the hall. 'That will be Sandra to tell me they're just leaving.' Joel thought as he walked through.

"Hello San ------------------.

"You've killed her haven't you? After I told you I didn't want to, you've gone and killed her."

"I've no idea what you're talking about Calypso." Joel lied, if Edenson had agreed to this place he may have tapped the phone.

"Hetty Betts, you've fucking killed her, haven't you heard the news? It's all over the TV and Radio."

'I haven't got a TV or a radio yet I didn't know.'

"Never ever contact me or speak to me again Joel." Calypso yelled down the phone between sobs.

The phone clicked off.

Joel poured the boiling water into the teapot. Hornimans, mum always liked Hornimans tea. What was good enough for her was good enough for him. He sat on the bed with the mug. 'Well Edenson would be pleased, and Sandra would never have to meet Calypso, every cloud has a silver lining.' He took a sip of tea. The phone rang again. He picked it up and said nothing.

"Hello you, it's me." Sandra's beautifully innocent voice poured oil over his troubled waters.

"We're just about to leave, all the stocks gone, I've shut the house down and we'll see you about two-ish this afternoon."

"How's your mum?" Joel asked.

"Quiet." It's taking a while to get over dad. This is a big change for her. I'm sure she'll be OK once we get settled and she gets to know you. I do appreciate you letting her live with us , you're such a love."

"I'll go into town and buy some stuff, that is if I can find anything open."

"Don't bother I've got a load of essentials in the back of the car, tomorrow we'll sit down and make out some lists of what we need. I love making lists."

"Where do I come on your list Sandra Hardwick?"

"At the very top, see you later." The phone clicked off. Nothing felt real.

The house slowly filled up, a table from this auction, some chairs from a second hand shop, an old wooden bed and a new mattress for mum. Sandra had very positive ideas of what she wanted and where it would go. Tablecloths, serviettes, new curtains, new towels, new bed linen, vases, flowers, china and cutlery began filling up the spaces.

"We need a more practical vehicle than my Mini." Joel said as he dropped the logs into the basket. "Your Volvo is OK but a Mini is next to useless, what do you think about an old Landrover?"

"Makes sense."

"The bloke who owns the garage at Marshbrook has one stuck round the back, it's an old nineteen fifties semi sidevalve but they go on forever. It's a pick-up as well, very useful."

"Dad always had a landrover before he bought a new Austin Champ, after he'd gotten used to it he used to say he preferred the 'Landy'."

"I'll go and see him tomorrow, see if he'll do a deal. We could do with a stock trailer as well, there's a farm auction at Little Stretton next Thursday, there's a Rice twin horse trailer in it. That would be very useful for the pigs and sheep."

"Can we afford it? We've spent a lot recently on the house and everything." Sandra's voice carried through from the kitchen. Kathleen was busy setting out the table. Her face morose and blank, her demeanour quiet and beaten as though nothing more could hurt her. She'd been with them for six months now, rarely speaking, never smiling.

"Yes." Joel said.

"This came in the post today, forgot to tell you."

Sandra handed him a plain A4 size manilla envelope postmarked London.

"What is it?" She asked.

Joel sat in the armchair Sandra had brought for him at Ludlow Antique Market and opened it.

"It's the title deeds to the farm. You keep them somewhere safe Sandra." Joel felt pleased Edenson had kept his side of the deal. Calypso, Bicknor and Hetty Betts were disappearing into the abyss of time. Leonard Flower Welham would never disappear, Saul Molloy or rather his impostor would. He usually rang Constantine Ellis every week.

"I thought this place was rented?"
"It was but now I've bought it."

Sandra came through with two plates of plaice, mashed potato peas and parsley sauce with a slice of lemon on the fish.
"Is it Friday then?"
"Yes, it comes after Thursday and before Saturday."
"Oh." Sandra returned to the kitchen for her mother's plate. Somehow she looked bigger. No, not bigger, just more 'rounded'

"You're a bit of a 'Mystery Man' Mr. Joel, how did you manage to buy it? Do we have a mortgage?"
"No, I had a bit of a win on Vernons football coupons."
"You don't do football coupons." Sandra admonished. Joel ignored her.

It was a beautiful summer's morning. The sun drenched everything in shining kisses, the breeze blew the kisses everywhere.

"Well you weren't wrong, it certainly is 'old'." Sandra stood at the door with Joel looking at the dark green Landrover.
"Yes but it does have a towbar."
"What does it run on? 'Paraffin?" Sandra joked.
"Just about. Come on let me take you 'round the fields in it."
"What year is it?" She asked as she clambered onto a red leatherette pad that pretended to be a passenger seat.
"Nineteen fifty one, we'll go and check on the sheep."
"Do you know what these yellow and red knobs do?" She asked.

"Of course, I'm a man." She thumped him in the ribs with her right ha
Landrover left the track for the rising grass bank.

"I looked at Flo and Maj yesterday, I saw Henry having a go at ther
back. I think they're 'in-pig' their 'tits' are getting bigger."

"They're 'teets' not tits'." Sandra paused. " And so are mine."

Joel pulled the Landrover to a halt on the grass. Two rabbits ran for the safety of the hedge.

"Really?" He looked at her.

"Really, and very tender as well."

"Have you told your mother?"

"Course not, far too early."

"Should we get one of those kits from the Chemists?"

"Next week when we go to the auction for that trailer."

"OK." Joel leant over and kissed her tenderly on her cheek. Sandra blushed for a second.

"Come on then let's check the sheep, hope that fox hasn't been back."

The Rice trailer fetched two hundred and eighteen pounds. The lights weren't working because the lead just before the plug had been dragged along the ground and some of the wires inside were chaffed and broken plus the aluminium plug housing was ground away on one side.

"The tyres are new, I reckon we've got a good bargain here Sandra, they're in the thousands new, especially a twin." Joel commented as he struggled with the rusty pilot wheel.

"Here let me help you, we'll just lift it up onto the hitch." Sandra said.

"Don't you touch it, not in your condition."

Sandra scowled at him.

"I'm not in any 'condition' . We haven't even bought a test kit yet."

"We're doing that on the way home." The trailer clunked down over the hitch.

"It's a heavy old thing, Do you think the Landy can handle it?"

"Course, that's what they're made for, jump in."

"The number on the back doesn't match our number."

"We'll risk it, tomorrow I'll sort the lights and get a number plate. What's your mum doing for supper tonight?"

" Stew and dumplings."

"It's high summer, that's a cold winter's night meal."

"Just be grateful Joel."

Joel started up the quiet engine and slipped off the handbrake. Whoever had the Landy before wasn't in the habit of pressing the button in before lifting the dle. The ratchet sounded quite weak, you could only just hear it. It made him think of Calypso.

Their bedroom was so peaceful, except for the chickens which crowed and shrieked at the slightest provocation. The small wooden windows opened up to let in the Long Mynd Hills, their colours, their movement, their music. Sandra had decorated the room beautifully in subtle cream paper with fielded roses. Burr walnut dressing table, chest of drawers and wardrobe she'd brought from Arrosmith. The big bed was soft and comfortable, it's down pillows cradling and soft. The polished oak floorboards somehow soaked up time and history, tears of both kinds undoubtedly soaked into their patina. There was no upstairs bathroom so a china pisspot hid under the bed.

It was four thirty a.m. when Sandra woke him. Just beginning to get light.

"It's blue, it's positive!" Her round red face was beaming, her frizzy hair disregarded.

Joel focussed his eyes and propped himself up.

"A boy or girl?"

"It doesn't tell you that." She hit him playfully. "It'll be a girl."

"How do you know that?"

"I just do, I'll tell mother today, hopefully it'll bring some joy back into her life."

Joel lay back onto his pillow and pushed the duvet away. Sandra went off into her mothers room.

'A father, he'd never been a father before, except of course for Janey's son but his real father was Keith so it wasn't the same. This was the real thing. Expect Sandra would be keen to decorate the small back bedroom out as a nursery, he'd paint it plain white just to make it clean, a sort of blank sheet of paper for Sandra to do her stuff on. The curtains were filthy, he'd take them down. He'd have to think about some heating for upstairs, you could get big straw bale burners, they seemed to be popular with farmers, they'd heat the whole house. Maybe a new big Rayburn, one that would heat upstairs as well. He wondered what name Sandra would like, she wouldn't like 'Calypso' that's for sure. No, it would be something traditional and sensible, her grandma was called 'Grace', I expect it would be that. I quite like Florentine, he thought to himself, no that was too close to 'Constantine' Sandra would think it odd, anyway she'd get called 'Flo' and that wasn't very nice. How about Judy or Judith after his mum, that could work.'

"Tea in bed?" Came the shout from downstairs.

"Yes please. Wow! It is a special day. We'll have to have some more babies."

"Shhhhhhhh You!" Mom will be listening.

Sandra bustled up the stairs with two mugs of tea, put one down on the carpet beside him then sat on the end of the bed. She made the room hot, her smile and happiness radiated from her.

"I want a cow?"

"Most people prefer to have a boy or a girl?"

"No silly, I think we ought to get a couple of Jerseys, just for the milk, just for our family, what do you think?"

"They're expensive and not very popular in Shropshire but we could look see."

Sandra got up and kissed him.

"Better get up and do the pigs and chickens Dad! I'll make us some breakfast."

"OK Mom!" They both laughed.

It was a satisfying routine, Joel saw to the chickens and pigs then came in for a breakfast that Sandra or her mum had cooked on the Rayburn. There were three Tamworths in the small orchard at the side of the house, they were doing a good job of turning over the old grass but now that Flo and Maj were 'in pig' he'd have to build a shelter. There was a pile of old stone around the back of the big barn, he'd try to use that. He'd never done any kind of building before. 'Surely it can't be that difficult', he thought to himself.

"Pass the butter love." Joel said.

"If we get a couple of Jersey heifers and get them in calf we can make our own butter and cheese, any excess milk we can sell in bottles to locals from the bottom gate."

"Isn't that illegal?" Joel asked between marmalade on toast and coffee.

"I expect so, everything good usually is. I'll look into it. When can we get them?"

"Blimey, talk about strike whilst the iron's hot, I don't know, we'll have to check out the markets. I'm off to Craven Arms now to get a new plug, some cable and a number plate for the trailer, do you want anything?"

"Get some cheese will you, some of that Glastonbury Cheddar from the little shop round the back."

"OK. Have you told your mum yet?"

"No, I'll do it today."

Joel enjoyed driving the 'Landy' it's crudeness and simplicity appealed to him. He didn't mind the draughts, rattles and bangs. You could drive it without having a shave or even cleaning your teeth. The roads were relatively empty, the summer leaves and flowers emptied his mind of winter thoughts.

"According to McCartney and Morris in this weeks 'Star' there's a big farm sale just outside Welshpool, a small herd of twelve Jersey cows it says."

"We're not buying a herd, that's a life sentence."

Sandra furrowed her brow and tut tutted him.

"No, but we could go and see if they're willing to sell us two. I'll ring them and find out."

"You only want them so we can have full cream Jersey milk for the baby."

"So."

"OK ring them."

Mum came into the room with some logs for the Rayburn, she seemed happier, the despondent set of her face was relaxing.

"I'm going to be a grandmother I hear." She said to Joel. He was surprised, she rarely spoke directly to him.

"Looks that way, yes, are you OK with that?"

"I'd be more OK if you were married."

"We're working on it."

"Well don't leave it too long she'll be showing in a couple of months then it looks bad."

"OK Mum." It was the first time he called Patricia Hardwicke 'Mum'.

Joel walked in with a large wedge of cheese wrapped in greaseproof paper. Sandra had a big grin on her face.

"I rang them and they said they would be prepared to sell us to heifers before the auction but they'd be at a premium price as we'd get the pick of the herd and then of course the herd would be smaller. The auctions in ten days time so we'd have to get our skates on. What do you think?"

"Will it make you happy?"

"Yes."

"Do you know anything about cows? You know, the difference between a good one and a not so good one?"

"Yes of course, I'm a farmer's daughter and a bloody vet, how much more knowledge do you want?"

"Only asking! Only asking! Ring them and say we'll go on Thursday morning, it'll give me time to get the trailer sorted."

"OK." Sandra came over, pressed her round body against him and kissed him.

"I'm taking mum shopping tomorrow to Shrewsbury."

"What for?"

"I don't know, she just says she wants to go. Says she's never been to Shrewsbury."

"Well that's a good sign, at least she's beginning to take an interest in things again instead of just moping around the house."

"She doesn't 'mope', she's very good, I couldn't manage without her. There's a lot to do."

"If you say so!"

Thursday morning was overcast but you could tell the sun would win come midday. The trailer looked spick and span, all the lights worked and the new number plate was where it should be.

"Don't worry about lunch mum, we'll get some chips in Welshpool." Sandra shouted as she closed the red door. They'd discussed changing the colour of the door but somehow it was just right.

"Got your cheque book Farmer Joel."

"You don't really love me do you? You just love my cheque book."

"I love a man with a big one." Sandra laughed. "It's so therapeutic signing cheques. I love it." The Little green Landrover and the big silver horse box pulled away from the gate of 'Bird on a Rock' Farm.

The road to Welshpool wound it's way gently down hill towards the main road that separated Newtown and Welshpool. Joel drove carefully to get the feel of towing the box.

"What are we going to do about getting married?" Joel asked on an empty stretch of road.

"Is that a formal proposal?" Sandra laughed.

"If you want it to be."

"Well I suppose it's the only proposal I'm likely to get."

"Stop putting yourself down, you're a wonderful intelligent caring person, I've never met anyone who comes close to you. Oh and I love you."

"I'll organise it as soon as we can at the Office in Welshpool, all you have to do is turn up with a ring and a Best Man if you have one. Can you manage that?"

"Is that a ring or a Best Man?"

"Both."

"I'll ask Connie and go to Woolworths."

"I thought he was a 'Spy' or something?"

"Only in his spare time, He's really a bookbinder."

"What's his proper name?"

"Constantine Ellis, very well to do family, quite well off."

"Where did you meet him? Turn right here, turn right here."

"At the rehab."

"Is he a druggie then?

"No."

From the tone of the 'no' Sandra knew not to ask anymore.

"We have to go through Welshpool and apparently it's about five miles up the Machynlleth road on the left. The chap has a white Ford Cortina, he'll wait by the McCartney 'For Sale' Sign."

"What's his name?"

"I don't know, I didn't ask."

He was young, tall, thin, with a barbour and a flat hat. His name was Thomas.

"She knows her cattle, your wife." He commented as Sandra perused, inspected and rejected several of the honey fawn beasts.

"She knows a lot of things my wife, so be careful, she's a vet."

Thomas glanced sideways at Joel and smiled.

"We'll take those two over there, the two standing together by the tree."

"Good choice." Thomas said.

"How do you know?" Sandra asked.

Thomas smiled.

"I'm a vet too, it's my day off and father manages the Welshpool Office. He's extremely busy today so he asked me to meet you."

"How can we pay?" Joel asked.

"Cheque will do nicely, two hundred and fifty pounds, you'll get a receipt in the post after the cheque's cleared."

"Two thirty for cash." Sandra butted in.

Thomas's eyes drifted between the two of them.

"Do you have that money with you?"

"Yes." Sandra said.

There was a cold Welsh pause.

"OK but you won't get a receipt."

"That's OK." Sandra said ,producing a tight roll of notes from the pocket of her coat. Sandra counted them out and handed them over. Thomas counted them, rolled them up and put them in his pocket. He shook hands with Joel and Sandra.

"Pleasure doing business with you, anytime in the future you need anything contact me direct." He handed over a card. Got into his cortina and left.

"What?" Sandra returned his look.

"I'm a farmer's daughter, what do you expect."

"Where did you get the money from?" Joel asked.

"Mum."

"So now we have to load up two Jersey Heifers from a field in the middle of nowhere, on our own with no receipt. The Police will be here before we know it."

"It's the middle of Wales Joel, there are no police, back the box up to the field gate."

There was a silence.

"You can back a trailer I presume?"

"Don't know, never tried."

"Oh for Gods sake, give me the keys. Go and put the reverse lock on the towbar." Sandra commanded. Joel looked vacant. Sandra looked at him.

"Right this little latch here stops the brakes of the box coming on when we want to reverse. Simple."

"OK, I get it, and we take it off for normal going forward?"

Sandra looked at him and smiled, almost laughed.

"God you're quick!"

"How do we get them in?"

"A head rope and a bucket of feed, come on."

The cattle were as meek and gentle as they looked, following the feed bucket up the tailboard and into the box. Sandra tied their head ropes to the rail and squoze out the side. Joel was waiting to swing up the tailgate.

"Might need the low range drive to get us out of this splay, it's a bit muddy and steep. Press the yellow knob down." Sandra instructed.

Joel pressed it to engage the lower gear range and crawled slowly but surely out onto the tarmac.

"Let me just check everything." Sandra swung out of the door and walked to the back, Everything was OK, the two cows were calm, munching at the hay net in front of them. She bounced back in, the thin bare door banging shut behind her.

"OK, let's go home. What about the chips?"

"We'll go past the chippy on the way through, if there's a place to pull in we'll stop, if there isn't we'll starve til we get home." Joel replied.

The Landrover and box cruised easily along the almost empty roads.

"If we do manage to stop, I want to nip into Boots to get some new toothbrushes, ours are all soft and useless."

"OK."

"Do you remember that song?"

"What song?" Joel asked as he dropped down to third for the hill.

"'The Toothbrush Song', Max Bygraves, surely you must.

'You're a pink toothbrush, I'm a blue toothbrush,
have we met somewhere before?
You're a pink toothbrush and I think toothbrush
that we met by the bathroom door.'

"Surely you must remember that? Every Saturday morning on Children's Favourites."

"No never heard it before, mind you, mum was more of a Joni Mitchell, Bob Dylan type of person if you get my drift."

"Mum loves Max Bygraves, 'Tulips from Amsterdam' and all that."

"When it's spring again,
I'll bring again,
Tulips from Amsterdam.
With a heart that's true,
I'll, give to you,
Tulips from Amsterdam. " - She sang in tune to the rattles and bumps of the Landrover. The wind from the half open sliding window blew her frizzy hair around her round reddish no makeup face, Joel thought how wonderful she looked.

"Sandra?"

"What?"

"If I were you I'd stick to farming."

She thumped his arm.

"Ow! That hurt!"

"Stop! Stop here! Look there's a big space there. Go there."

Joel pulled in and pulled on the handbrake, pressing the button in.

"Cod and chips, lots of vinegar and mushy peas please."
"Yes Madam, any preference of newspaper?"
"Yes it has to be in a 'Farmers Weekly."

Joel leant over and kissed her.

"Your wish is my command Ma'am." He laughed and slipped out of the driver's door.

They were delicious, somehow fish and chips from a chip shop always tasted better.

"OK, next stop 'Bird on a Rock' Farm." Joel started up the engine as Sandra climbed in with her Boots bag.

"I forgot to tell you in all the excitement, Connie's coming to visit next month, just for a weekend, says he wants to know what a Shropshire farmer's wife looks like?"
"Well he'll be disappointed then. We're not married."
"Thought you were working on it?"
"I am."

It took over an hour to drive carefully back to the farm. Sandra got out and opened the gate, standing by it and waving him through. It was a tight squeeze with the angle the box came in at. Joel drove up into the large wide yard and did a full sweeping turn before poking his head out of the window. Mum was standing at the front door watching them, waiting to see the cows.

"I'll have a go at backing up Sandra, put the lock on will you?"
Sandra slipped the latch across.

"OK." She shouted.

It took Joel about ten yards to twig that it was all or nothing with reversing a trailer, either it was a tiny correction of the steering wheel or the opposite lock.

"Hey that's not bad for a 'pretty boy'. Steady at that, come back another two yards."

Joel could smell the clutch getting hot as he pushed the box back up the incline towards the entrance to the big barn. The plan was to house them in there for a couple of days so they got used to them then turn them out to the summer pasture high up on the hill. 'He'd get Bryan at the garage to change the clutch next week, just as a precaution.' He thought to himself.

"Ok! That'll do." Sandra shouted as she unclipped the tailgate, it's big coil springs banging it down onto the grassy cobble of the yard. She picked up the now empty feed bucket and refilled it from the sack just inside the barn door. Joel went inside the house to use the toilet. He loved vinegar, but it didn't love him.

The two cows were almost identical. Sandra pushed them together so she could slip by to the front of the box, they both tried to push into the bucket, she untied the nearest cow and gently pushed the other one out of the bucket, then slowly pushed the bucket and the munching heifer backwards down the ramp. Once out she turned her and led her into the barn, 'One down, one to go.' She thought.

Chapter 19.

Mum was watching at the door.

"Put the kettle on mum. I'll be in in a minute." Sandra shouted. Pat disappeared into the house. The gentle Jersey needed no encouragement to tuck into the bucket. Sandra untied the head rope then there was a loose 'CLUNK' sound from the front, a barely perceptible movement increased rapidly as the tailboard bounced along the cobbles

"MUM! JOEL! WHAT'S HAPPENING?" She screamed.

The Landrover and trailer were now rolling down the yard, increasing in uncontrolled speed with every yard. The cow moved, she couldn't get past it. 'For God's sake what was happening?'

Then there was a huge bang and jolt as the Landover half climbed the stone wall to the left of the gate before coming to a halt. The box twisted to the left and toppled on it's side lifting the right hand rear wheel of the Landover high into the air. The impact with the ground collapsed the side and roof of the box into a tent ridge as the cow was thrown sideways onto Sandra.

Mother stood transfixed at the doorway as she heard her daughter utter a terrible moaning UGGGGGGGGGHHHHHHHHHHHHHH as the cow kicked at the floor of the box unable to move or get up.

"JOEL! JOEL! Come quick, something terribles happened!"

Joel rushed from the bathroom doing up his belt.

"Phone 999 mother quick, an ambulance and fire engine! Quick! Quick! Oh God NO! Please let her be safe!"

Joel rushed down to the box, the cow was on it's side on top of Sandra. The box was too squashed for the cow to get up. Sandra's legs were sticking out from under the cow. He tried to pull them, pull her out from underneath the cow but couldn't. He tried pulling the cow out by it's back legs but the animal was too heavy and kept kicking.

Patricia Hardwicke came down to the horse box. She was remarkably calm.

"That's no good, and God isn't going to help you. There's some rope in the barn, I'll get that and tie up the cow's back legs, you go into the house, get the keys to the Volvo and back it up." It was though the youthful power and confidence of Sandra had entered her mother. Joel rushed into the house.

The old blue Volvo easily pulled the cow out of the box. Sandra's lifeless body came partially with it. However much Joel implored her there was no movement, sound or response from Sandra. She lay in his arms, her beautiful red face was now horribly white, she was asleep or unconscious, or maybe in a coma but not dead.

" Please God, not dead!" 'What about Grace inside her?' His thoughts panicked. "Please! Please! If there is a God? Not dead Please!" Uncontrollable tears dropped onto her face. "Please God! Please God."

Joel was cradling her in his arms when the ambulance turned up, the man and woman crew gently easing him away so that they could check for signs of life. There were none. Pat knew it, she'd known it from the first and final sound she'd heard from her daughter. She was a farmer's wife, she knew about death. Joel wouldn't, couldn't accept it. "Not again? Please not again?"

The volunteer fire crew and their engine turned up. The six men easily pushed the distorted horsebox back onto it's wheels then backed the landrover back off the wall. No one spoke, they'd done as much as they could, they spoke to mother then left. That evening Derrick Cebo the local 'Bobby' came and quietly drove away the Landrover for inspection.

It was as though her death had reduced them to autonomous 'things', doing necessary chores with no joy, no pleasure, no satisfaction, nothing. Conversation was just mechanical, pragmatic, essential, there was no banter, no comments. Still it was better than being on your own. There were a lot of quiet moments when they both sat in the kitchen staring at the Rayburn waiting for it to require attention, another log, a poke about or an adjustment to the air flap. All the other chores were done, everything was done, anything was done to fill the empty space. Joel had been thinking about it for days, whether to do it within her earshot or not. She might get the wrong impression. He decided it didn't matter.

"Hi Connie, it's me."
"Hello, long time no hear. I was beginning to worry."

Joel's breathing became short and strained.

"What on earth's the matter are you ill?" Connie asked.
"No, I'm not ill, there's been a terrible accident here at the farm. A tragedy and I'm not coping at all well with it."

Constantine allowed a long silence as he sensed Joel getting himself together.

"Tell me about it, but only if you want to, if you feel up to it."
"I've got to talk to someone Constantine or I'll go mad and do something silly."
"Don't do anything silly, just tell me."
"Sandra's been killed in an accident, here in the farmyard and it's my fault. We bought an old Landrover, I set the handbrake but didn't leave it in gear, the handbrake jumped off, anyway Sandra got crushed by a cow in a trailer behind the Landrover and died, according to the Ambulance man almost instantly it would seem."

Joel could sense Pat listening.

"I'm coming over, right now, give me the address."

"No. No, please don't, there's absolutely nothing you can do and Sandra's mother is here living at the farm, you'd have to sleep in our bed and I don't want that."

"I could support you, offer a friendly ear, hold your hand so to speak, get you through it."

"I'll never get through it Connie, Sandra was five months pregnant, we'd settled on the name Grace."

"I want to put my arms around you and make it all better for you Joel."

"You can't Connie, no one can. I'm going now. I'll ring you next week when I know more about the funeral, will you come for that?"

"Of course."

"I'm thinking of having her buried in the orchard at the side of the house, we've got pigs in it now turning it over, the plan was half of it was to be a vegetable garden, the other half a small pony paddock for Grace."

"Is that allowed, is it legal?"

"Yes. Bye."

"Bye, you'll always have my love, you know that."

"Yes Thanks Connie."

Joel hoped that Pat hadn't heard the last bit.

The cow that had crushed Sandra to death was fine. They were both now in the top pasture as planned. Tomorrow was the Coroners inquest, it was only ten days ago they'd been eating fish and chips and singing, now he was dressing in black clothes.

"In the case of the sudden death of Ms. Sandra Elaine Hardwicke of 'Bird on a Rock Farm Clungunford Shropshire on the fifth of May Nineteen Sixty Six. It has been found that the handbrake ratchet mechanism of Landrover 64 SCJ was worn and when subjected to vibration caused by animal movement in an attached stock trailer it failed. Ms Hardwicke was subsequently crushed by a falling cow as the stock trailer overturned following it's uncontrolled descent into a stone wall. An autopsy has revealed that Ms Hardwicke sustained several broken ribs, one of which severed a major artery in the heart. Death would have been almost instantaneous. I therefore find that Ms. Sandra Elaine Hardwicke was subject to an accidental death. Ms Hardwicke was five months pregnant at the time with a female foetus, unfortunately life was unstainable at that stage of development."

The elderly Coroner stopped and took off his glasses and put them down on the desk. There were only five people in the room. Joel, Pat Hardwicke, a young reporter from the Shropshire Star, and Derrick Cebo, whose report the coroner had accepted.

"I'm so sorry, I believe you were about to be married Mr. Joel and I'm also aware Mrs. Hardwicke that you have recently lost your husband, Sandra's father to cancer. It must be a terrible time for you both. Please allow me to offer my sincerest condolences." The Coroner left his desk and shook Joel's and Pat's hands, his sympathy was real.

The short journey back from Shrewsbury to Clungunford was mostly in silence. Joel was driving on autopilot his thoughts with Sandra. She took care of everything, took charge of him, told him what to do, She was everything. How could he go on now? Go on without her? What the fuck for? There was no point to anything. Pat's face had now resumed the passive blank blotting paper it had been when she had first come here, absorbing everything bad the world could throw at her and just letting it spread over her.

"I want to bury Sandra and Grace in the side orchard. How do you feel about that? I want to be with them forever, I never want to leave them." Joel said. Tears streaming down his face.

There was nothing for a long time.

"I'm OK with that but how do you feel about living with an old woman in the house? Won't it cramp your style a bit?"

"I've never considered that you wouldn't be here. Sandra would expect that of me. Anyway I need your company, your friendship, your help."

"I'll put Christopher's funeral urn in with them." Was all she said. It was the first time he heard her use Sandra's dad's first name.

The funeral was very simple. Sandra would have approved, no fuss or bother. As instructed, the gravediggers had dug a very deep hole under the apple tree in the corner of the orchard. Connie had arrived the day before. Pat had immediately taken a liking to him as his presence lit up the room. Some friends from Arrowsmith and the Vets that Sandra had worked for also came. In all there were about twelve people collected around the grave on a blustery chilly morning that was always threatening rain. A single black Humber hearse with the Vicar sat in the front seat arrived exactly at eleven o'clock. It was just a plain pine coffin with a tiny plain pine coffin on top. Everybody was crying. Six of the men shouldered her coffin. The undertaker handed the tiny wooden box to Joel. He'd never seen his daughter. The undertaker asked him if he wanted to look.

Shaking and trembling, eyes sodden with tears Joel nodded, and there she was, tiny but perfect, a round pink face with traces of ginger hair, so peaceful, so exquisite. Joel nodded and the man closed the lid.

Sandra was lowered into her grave, Grace's casket was lowered gently on top. Pat's face was ashen as she lowered her husband's urn onto the coffin next to his granddaughter. The vicar's vestments flapped around him in the uncaring wind as he delivered a beautiful eulogy. Then it was done.

Pat had made sandwiches and cakes, there were drinks and snacks. Everyone was very polite then they drifted away. Connie was the last to leave. Holding Joel's hand in comfort as they walked towards the Bristol.

"Come to Oxford, take a break from here, it will do you good. You need it." Connie said.
"I will but not just yet, I have to look after Pat and the Farm. When are you going to Beirut?"
"Not til January next year."
"There's plenty of time then. I will come, promise." Joel kissed him on the cheek.

Joel and Pat sat silently in front of the Rayburn and the television.

"There's plenty of sandwiches left if you're hungry." Pat said.
"Thanks but I'm not."

It was ten thirty, proper darkness had only just arrived.

"Where are you going?" Pat asked as Joel rose and headed for the door.
"Say goodnight to Sandra."
"Oh. What about Grace?"
"She's fast asleep upstairs bless her."

Pat said nothing.

"I want a pair of curtains, this size with this type of hook."

The 'Busy Bee' was a small haberdashers in Craven arms, it's door was mainly glass but what wasn't was painted yellow and black.

"What colour fabric, plain or patterned?"
"Black just plain black."

The rather fat short woman looked at him strangely over her pink and white glasses.

"Black?"
"Yes Black."

She looked at the measurements again.

"That will be three pounds, ready Thursday next week."

Joel paid and left. The door had a little bell on it.

Joel and Pat worked hard and mostly silently on the farm. He couldn't bring himself to drive the Landrover or use the box. Bryan at the garage kindly agreed to take it back and found him a little Haflinger, it wasn't fast but it could go anywhere in any conditions. He collected the curtains. He'd parked near the fish and chip shop. Everything, absolutely everything reminded him of her. He was really hungry, they smelt really delicious but he couldn't do it.

"What are you doing upstairs?" Pat shouted up the tight winding staircase.
"Putting up curtains."
"Oh." She wondered where and also why.

It was an easy fix, Joel just clipped them up to the original rail. The room was white with a plain white wood dropside cot. He drew the curtains, shutting out all the light. He looked around it before shutting the door, it reminded him of the time when he was in bed with Calypso arguing over lyrics. 'In THE White Room, with black curtains, near the station.' He hummed the tune as he closed the door.

"Don't worry Grace it's miles away from the station, the trains won't disturb you." He said to her. "I'll get one of those little pot nameplates tomorrow with your name on and put it on your door. You'll like that won't you? Go straight to sleep mind. Daddy loves you very much."

Pat was out when he went downstairs, probably doing the chickens and pigs. He hadn't spoken to any other person other than Pat for days. His wallet was on the table, a bent and crumpled corner of a card stuck out. The old Biro writing was beginning to yellow and fade. Joel rang the number.

"Yes." A rather angry voice answered.
"Ms. Calypso please." 'It was a long shot but you never know.'
"Not available." Joel could sense the phone was about to go down.

"Don't go! Please don't go, can you take down my number and ask her to call me? Please."

"What is it?"

"Clunbury 573, the code is 0874."

"What's your name?"

"Joel, Mr. Joel, we're old friends."

"They all say that." The phone clicked down.

Joel went over, checked the Rayburn and put another log in. Pat came in the door.

"We need some more chicken pellets." She said.

"I'll get some from Church Stretton tomorrow, they're cheaper there. I'm going there anyway to get a name plate for Grace's room."

Pat didn't know what to say so she said nothing.

The phone rang. Joel looked at Pat before he moved quickly to the hall, he didn't want Pat to get it.

"Hello!." He was trembling a little bit. Had she forgiven him?

"Ah! Mr. Joel, Edenson here, I trust you're well and not too busy --------- ----------------------------------. "

The End.

Printed in Great Britain
by Amazon